The
STORMY
Life

of
Scarlett
Fife

ILLUSTRATED BY CHRIS JEVONS

Also by
MaZ EVanS:

Who Let the Gods Out?

Simply the Quest

Beyond the Odyssey

Against all Gods

Vi Spy: Licence to Chill

Vi Spy: Never Say Whatever Again

Vi Spy: The Girl with the Golden Gran

And look out for more books

about Scarlett Fife:

The **EXPLODING LifE** of *Scarlett Fife*
The **WOBBLY LifE** of *Scarlett Fife*

For

Ashley Booth
Steph Elliott
Scott Evans
Christopher Harrison
Ian Hunt

And all the incredible educators who have shared
their BIG FEELINGS about my books.

I am so grateful, I could explode.
Love and thanks to you all.

And in loving memory of
Audrey Andrews (or as I knew her)

Grandma

xxx

HODDER CHILDREN'S BOOKS

First published in Great Britain in 2023 by Hodder & Stoughton

1 3 5 7 9 10 8 6 4 2

A CIP catalogue record for this book
is available from the British Library.

ISBN 978 1 444 95780 8

Printed and bound in Great Britain by
Clays Ltd, Elcograf S.p.A.

The paper and board used in this book
are made from wood from responsible sources.

Hodder Children's Books
An imprint of
Hachette Children's Group
Part of Hodder & Stoughton Limited
Carmelite House
50 Victoria Embankment
London EC4Y 0DZ

An Hachette UK Company
www.hachette.co.uk

www.hachettechildrens.co.uk

Scarlett

Maisie

Polly

Ms Pitt-Bull

Aunty Amara

Aunty Rosa

William U and his mum

Emmeline

Jakub

Unimingo Power!

Gran

Rita

Bruce

CHAPTER I X I

I am not going to cry.

Here is a graph of all the reasons I don't like crying:

Puffy eyes
Snotty
It's for babies
Red face

(By the way, why do people cry when they're happy? You don't laugh when you're sad or scream when you're embarrassed. Don't be so greedy, crying, you only get one BIG FEELING.)

I don't cry.

I don't like crying.

I don't want to cry.

I'm not going to cry.

There have been lots of reasons I could have cried lately, but I haven't. Because I am Scarlett Fife. And Scarlett Fife (*that's me, by the way*) Does. Not. Cry. In fact, there are so many things I haven't cried about, I'm going to make a list:

Things I Haven't Cried About

1) Miss Hugg ISN'T coming back to my school, St Lidwina's

This is properly rubbish news. Miss Hugg is the BEST teacher ever. She once told us that she became a teacher because she really likes children, so I have no idea why she's decided to leave us and stay at home with her new baby all day. This means we have Ms Pitt-Bull 'permanently' (*which means until Year 6*), which isn't so bad as I like her now, but it's a bit like when you order chocolate ice cream for pudding in a restaurant and all they have is vanilla. It's still ice cream. It's just not the one you really wanted.

2) William U IS coming back to my school, St Lidwina's!!!

Now, this one I have lots of **BIG FEELINGS** about. William U left St Lidwina's to go to his private school, but now he's not being very private at all and he's coming back! And his old school didn't teach him to be any less of a pain either – he's still SUPER annoying. William U's mum is back as well. She used to be our teaching assistant, but Ms Pitt-Bull let out **BIG FEELINGS** about that to whoever was head teacher that day.

So now William U's mum is not our teaching assistant, which is the only good thing. But she IS a playground supervisor, so we *still* have to see her every day, and she can *still* see What's Upsetting William (*which is everything, by the way, because William U is a pain in the rear end. Which is the same as 'bum', but I'm trying to use Polite Olden Days words, instead of fart, wee, poo and stuff*).

3) Leaving my old house

Six weeks ago, we moved to our new house in Lady Tottington-Snoot's garden because Jakub has started his rubbish new job (*see below*). The new house is great, but saying goodbye to my old house made me very sad. I said goodbye to every room and every window and every door and every flower in the garden. Then Mum said I had to stop saying goodbye to everything because the new people wanted to get inside their new home. But even though I was very sad because it's the only home I've ever known except for Dad's house, Aunty Rosa and Aunty Amara's house and Granny's house, I DID NOT CRY!!

4) Jakub's rubbish new job (I told you)

I *was* very happy when Jakub got his dream job working for Lady Tottington-Snoot as her groundskeeper. But I'm not happy now. Jakub has to work all day and lots of the weekend and we can't do ANY of the fun stuff we used to do. Mum says it's really great that he's In A Good Place, but I'd rather be In A Better Place like Wet and Wacky at the swimming pool on Saturdays. (*By the way, my mum is now SUPER ENORMOUS with two babies in her tummy and she can hardly walk, let alone take me to Wet and Wacky. I think if she tried to go down the waterslides now, she'd get stuck and they'd have to rescue her, just like they did William*

D's dad when his swimming trunks went down the chute without him and he had to hold himself inside the Blue Lagoon because he didn't want everyone to see his rear end.)

5) Maisie

Until today, this was the actual worst one. Maisie, my School BFF might be moving away (*her, me and Polly decided that Maisie was going to be my School BFF and Polly was going to be my Home BFF, by the way, because that's the best way to organise it all now Polly's mum Rita has moved in with my dad*). Maisie's foster family is moving to Australia and Maisie can't go with them. I'm very glad she's not going to Australia, because it's a whole day away and then she'd be on Wednesday when I'm only on Tuesday and we'd never be on the same day. But she will have to go to a new foster family – and they might not live near here, which means Maisie would have to move house AND school. If I was the sort of person who cried, this would be the sort of thing I'd cry about. But I'm not.

So you see? Even with ALL those reasons to cry, I didn't.

So I'm not going to cry today.

Even though when I came down for breakfast this morning, my mum and Aunty Rosa and Aunty Amara and Jakub were all crying.

Even though they told me that my granny was taken to hospital last night.

Even though my granny had to be put to sleep to have an operation to fix her heart.

Even though my granny never woke up.

Even though I'm never going to see my granny again.

I.
Am.
NOT.
Going.
To.
Cry.

CHAPTER 2 – 2 + 2

The reason I like numbers at least fifty-two times more than I like words is because numbers always do the right thing, but words don't. What's the word for something that catches fire really easily?

Flammable.

So 'inflammable' should mean the opposite – something that doesn't catch fire easily, right? (*'Right', by the way, is a word that can mean 1) not wrong, 2) not left, 3) something that means you can do something and 4) 'look how right I am about the silly words flammable and inflammable'.*)

Wrong!

(*That just means 'wrong', to be fair.*)

Inflammable means something that catches

fire really easily! This makes literally, actually NO sense at all! All the other 'in-' words are an opposite – inconsiderate, indecisive, intelligent (*that one isn't an opposite, by the way, but Granny always said that 'the exception proves the rule', just like when she said she wasn't going to drink ANY wine in January, except when it was a Thursday and she wanted to*). I call silly words that make no sense Unwords, because they are silly and make no sense.

Another silly Unword is the word 'wake'. Wake usually means something you do every morning after you've been asleep.

So it's a really silly Unword for a party for someone who won't wake up tomorrow, or any other morning ever.

Today it's Granny's wake. The grown-ups have been to her funeral at the church, but I didn't go because they said it would be too upsetting for me. This made no sense, because I'm very upset already. But Rita offered to take me, Maisie and Polly bowling instead and I did slightly prefer being upset with a hot dog, blue slushy and two pounds to play on the arcade machines.

Now we are all at Granny's house and everyone is in her garden as it's a nice sunny day. I'm glad about that – Granny hated the rain and she loved gardening, so this is the best place to be. Although it would be so much better if she was here digging in the dirt and complaining about 'all these blasted weeds'.

I am NOT going to cry.

Crying is a **BIG FEELING** that I don't like. I keep feeling The Crying trying to come out of my throat, but I won't let it.

I look over at Rita, Polly, Aunty Amara and Maisie doing cartwheels on the grass. It looks super fun, but I didn't want to join in because it doesn't feel right having fun at my granny's wake, when my granny won't ever wake up or have any fun ever again. Rita and Polly are both really good at cartwheels (*Polly does gymnastics on Wednesdays, by the way, and she can do all kinds of stuff AND she gets to wear a blue leotard with stars on it. I tried it, but I Found Gymnastics a Challenge and was only really good at wearing the leotard, so I just kept that and didn't do the cartwheels any more*). But Aunty Amara and Maisie aren't very good at cartwheels, so they are lying on the floor laughing so hard, they're breathing funny. Aunty Amara pulls Maisie in for a giant hug. I haven't told my family about Maisie going yet, because I'm hoping that if I don't tell them it won't come true.

I pick up a jam sandwich. Because everyone is too sad to cook, we have something called Caterers, who have done all the cooking and made lots of yummy cakes and sandwiches – I'm definitely going to get them to come and do all my cooking when I'm sad because they're really good. I bet if I put some more jam sandwiches in my throat, The

Crying won't be able to come out. It's been working really well so far today.

Mum and Aunty Rosa are sitting at a table while Jakub and Dad take sandwiches round the guests. I'm going to go and sit with them. Jakub says they will need my love and support today as they've lost their mum. And they're also closest to the cakes.

'... but you must be relieved,' Mum says to Aunty Rosa as I come up behind them. 'With all the paperwork done, surely it won't be long now ...'

I stop.

Paperwork?

Paperwork is never a good thing. Grown-ups get grumpy and stressed about paperwork. I learned lots of new Bad Choice Words when Mum and Jakub sold our old house and there was LOADS of paperwork. Maybe Aunty Rosa is moving from her Big Posh House? Maybe she's moving to an Even Bigger, Posher House? That could be fun ...

'We have our last meeting on Monday,' sighs Aunty Rosa, picking up her wine. 'Although even if everything goes according to plan, it could still be weeks before everything is finalised and we can get on with our lives.'

Oh no.

I've heard this kind of talking once before.

The last time my family needed paperwork to be 'finalised' so we could all 'get on with our lives'.

The time my mum and dad got divorced.

I'm feeling sicky and panicky and sad all at once. Aunty Rosa and Aunty Amara can't get divorced –

they're in love. They're a family. They have a really Big Posh House …

Wait a minute! Aunty Rosa is a lawyer! She does paperwork all the time! She must be talking about her job …

'Is Amara ready?' my mum asks. 'It'll be a big change for you both.'

'This was all Amara's idea,' says Aunty Rosa. 'She can't wait. Tomorrow isn't soon enough for her.'

Oh. So it's not Aunty Rosa's job.

'And you?' my mum asks. 'Are you ready?'

Aunty Rosa tries to smile.

'I will be,' she says. 'When it finally happens. It's the right thing for us. It's just hard to think of anything at the moment. Anything apart from …'

'I know,' says Mum, quickly putting some cake on top of her crying. 'Me too.'

Oh no.

I was right.

My aunties are getting a divorce.

Just like Mum and Dad.

I walk quietly backwards and back into the house. I feel The Crying coming up in my throat and I haven't got any cake to squash it with – so I shut my eyes and swallow really hard instead to push it back inside me. I can't believe it. Aunty Amara and Aunty Rosa are splitting up. This is the worst wake ever.

I run upstairs to my room at Granny's house and throw myself on to the bed. Then I get up and take my shoes off (*Granny really didn't like shoes on the bed, by the way*), then I throw myself back on it again. I don't like this. I don't like any of it. I've already lost my granny. I don't want to lose my Aunty Amara as well.

I bury my head in the pillow and swallow hard and push The Crying down. But it's not working very well as I'm so sad and I'm worried.

But suddenly there is a knock at the door.

'Scarlett?' my mum says. 'Can I come in?'

I want to say no. But I'm not sure why, because I really want my mum. So I change my mind.

'Yes,' I say, and Mum opens the door. She's been crying a lot. Her cake obviously didn't work as well as mine. She sits down on the bed next to me. Because she's very full of babies now, she nearly bounces me off the bed, but I stay there.

'How are you doing?' Mum asks.

'Really rubbish,' I say, because I am and I don't see any point lying about it.

Mum laughs a bit and holds me to her.

'Me too,' she says in her crying voice. I can feel her snotty tears in my hair. The babies are kicking in her tummy. Maybe she's crying snotty tears all over them too. She sits up and wipes her eyes.

'Before Granny had her operation,' says Mum, pulling open the drawer next to my bed, 'she wrote

letters to us all in case … in case she didn't wake up.'

Oh! So that's why this is called a wake? To make sure Granny woke up at least one more time. That makes much more sense. Perhaps it's not such a silly Unword after all.

Mum sniffs and breathes funny. It's making me want to cry. I take it back – cake is no good at stopping The Crying.

'This … this is the one she wrote to you,' says Mum, reaching into the drawer. 'I thought you might like it today.'

Mum takes something out of the drawer – it is a small parcel with an envelope stuck to it.

And it's got my name on it.

In Granny's handwriting.

I wipe the not-tears from the eyes that weren't crying and take it from my mum. It's addressed to me.

'Can I open it?' I ask, which is a bit silly because it's addressed to me, so it's really up to me whether I open it or not.

'Of course,' says Mum, standing up (*which takes a while, by the way, because really she's standing up for three people so it takes about three times as long*). 'I'll leave you to enjoy it in peace.'

She kisses my head and waddles out of the door.

I turn the parcel round and gently open a corner of the envelope. But that doesn't work, so I just rip it open. I check the envelope for money – Dad says you should always check the envelope

for money – but all that is inside is a letter on Granny's posh writing paper. Granny always said she didn't believe in emails (*which was weird, by the way, as she had a computer with loads of them on it, so the proof they existed was right there in her office*) and that she much preferred the handwritten word. She also had very strong opinions about the right sort of paper and pens, but I usually stopped listening at that point and asked her for some sweets instead.

But this is some of Granny's posh writing paper, the stuff that smells of flowers. I smell the letter. It smells just like Granny ...

I am NOT going to cry.

I unfold the letter and start to read it. I've actually unfolded it upside down, so it doesn't make much sense, but when I turn it the right way around, this is what it says:

Darling Scarlett,

I hope you are well. I have a job for you to do.

(Although Granny preferred the handwritten word, she didn't like to use too much of it, by the way.)

I know that everyone will deal with me not being here in their own way. But I also know that it's important that they do deal with it somehow. I can think of no better person to make sure this happens than you.

I want you to make a Memory Book out of the enclosed parcel. I want you to go around our family and get a special memory from them — it can be a picture or a story or whatever they want — and I want you to stick all the memories in this book. I think it will help everyone. And it makes me happy to think of this book full of happy memories of me.

You're going to be fine. Always remember,

my lovely girl, there is nothing wrong with your BIG FEELINGS. They are merely a wonderful product of your Big Heart.

Now, chop chop (*Granny always said this, by the way*) – you have a job to do.

I love you, Scarlett.

Love,

Granny

I open the parcel and a small gold book with black pages falls out of it. It's really pretty. And very practical. Just like my granny.

I can hear laughing in the garden below and go and stand by the window. Jakub is saying something about Granny that is making Mum and my aunties laugh. Dad is hugging Rita and Polly, and Maisie is sitting on Aunty Rosa's lap being tickled. This would make a nice memory.

I look at the book in my hand. A Memory

Book. That's a really good idea. Granny always had the best ideas. And she was the only grown-up who knew about my BIG FEELINGS. And she always knew what to do when I didn't.

I feel The Crying come up my throat, but I am NOT going to cry. It's coming up really fast, so I swallow as hard as I can so it can't come out. I look out of the window to think about something else – but instead of the nice sunshiny day, there's now a massive black storm cloud filling the sky. Where did that come from? But I don't have time to worry about the rain as The Crying is still trying to come out and so I close my eyes and push the tears back down and I'm not sure if I can stop them because they're really strong and—

KER-BOOM!

A huge clap of thunder suddenly rings out across the garden. I open my eyes and look down at the wake. The storm cloud is pouring with rain

and everyone's having to run inside before they get wet – everyone except for Aunty Amara and Maisie and Polly, who are dancing in the rain. I hope that someone remembers to bring the cakes and sandwiches – the Caterers will be sad if all their lovely food gets spoiled. And I really want another jam sandwich.

That was weird, though. I don't understand. Just a moment ago it was warm and sunny and then out of nowhere this big storm cloud comes and rains on everyone ...

Uh-oh.

I know what's going on.

My **BIG FEELINGS.**

It's happening again.

I'm making weird stuff happen.

And this time I don't have my granny to help me.

ChaPTER 9 ÷ 3

Having Polly at Dad's house is SUPER awesome
because:

   1) We share a bedroom

   2) We can watch *UniMingoes* every day

   3) Rita is a brilliant cook and we get really nice
food that isn't always Something On Toast like my
dad makes

When Polly moved in, I told her all about my
BIG FEELINGS and how when I worry, things
wobble, and when I get angry, things explode. At
first she didn't believe me – but then I got cross
about only getting fifty-five per cent in a Maths

test (*on percentages*) and blew up a bowl of rice pudding, which showed her that I was telling the truth (*even though, by the way, I'd already crossed my heart and sworn to stick a sausage in my eye if I was lying, which should really have been enough for my Home BFF*).

'So you think that *you* made the storm cloud come? And rain on everyone?' says Polly as we sit on the swings in Dad's garden.

I nod my head. I don't even want to say it out loud. Polly wrinkles her nose. She does this when she's having a really good think.

'Are you still crying a lot?' she asks. 'Because that's okay when someone dies.'

'No,' I say. 'I never cry. I don't like it.'

'Well, maybe you should try it,' she shrugs. 'I cried all the time when my dad died. I still do sometimes.'

'But ... isn't crying a bit ... babyish?' I ask, not

wanting to hurt Polly's feelings.

'My mum says that crying is one of the bravest things you can do,' Polly replies, jumping off the swing and picking up my pink Frisbee. 'It takes real courage to show how you feel. Think about our last head teacher, Ms Poke, who got up in front of all the parents and children and teachers at the Spring Concert and told them that St Lidwina's was a "disgrace that lacked proper management".'

'But Ms Poke was asked to leave our school in the interval by the School Governors. I saw her crying when I was buying my crisps and fizzy pop.'

'Exactly!' says Polly. 'If it's okay for grown-ups to cry, it's okay for us. So why don't you just have a good cry?'

I nod, but I don't tell her the biggest answer, the one that has been shouting in my tummy and my heart and I won't let it shout out of my mouth.

Yes, crying is babyish and makes you snotty.

But there's another, really good reason I don't want to cry.

Because if I start, I'm scared I won't ever stop.

'Wanna play?' says Polly.

'Er … maybe later,' I say. It still doesn't feel right to have a good time when my granny isn't here any more.

'Come on!' Polly insists, pulling me up off my swing. 'I can't play Frisbee all by myself.'

'Okay, okay,' I groan, trudging down to the other end of the garden. Before Granny died, I did think it was much better having someone else to play with. Polly's right, Frisbee isn't a lot of fun on your own (*just like swingball, throw and catch, and especially*

hide and seek, by the way, because no matter how high I counted, I always knew where I had hidden).

We start to throw the Frisbee – we're both still a bit rubbish at it, so we laugh and squeal a lot whenever it comes near us. For a minute, I forget to feel bad that my granny has died. I give the Frisbee a really hard throw and Polly screams as it whooshes towards her head. It makes me laugh even harder and I'm just about to scream as she throws it back at me, when a Big Loud Voice nearly makes me jump like a rubber frog (*that's a simile, by the way, which is when you use 'like' or 'as' to say something is like something else, even though it's not. I don't really understand why it's a good thing to say something is 'as' or 'like' something else it's not, but Ms Pitt-Bull gave me a sparkly sticker for using a simile in my story about a singing carrot the other day, so I'm going to use them more*).

'WILL YOU KEEP THE NOISE DOWN

OVER THERE! IT'S LIKE LIVING NEXT TO
A RUDDY ZOO!'

(*'Ruddy' is a Polite Olden Days Bad Choice Word,
by the way – my granny used to say it about people
who sell things at the door and wasps.*)

Polly and I turn to see where the Big Loud Voice
is coming from, which is really bad timing as it
means that I completely miss the Frisbee, which
whizzes over into next door's garden.

'Oooops!' I squeal as I look over Elsie's fence.
Elsie is the really nice lady who lives next door to
my dad. She's quite old, but she always throws my
stuff back over the fence and makes really nice cakes
like a really nice neighbour. (*That's not a simile, by
the way, she's actually just a really nice neighbour.*)

But Really Nice Elsie isn't standing over her
fence with a Really Nice Cake. Instead, it's a
Really Grumpy Man standing over her fence with
a Really Grumpy Face.

'I won't tell you again – keep it down!' he shouts at us. 'Have some consideration for other people! I don't want to hear you caterwauling like a pack of hyenas!'

'That's a very good simile,' I tell him, hoping it might make him a bit less grumpy. I don't tell him that we weren't actually putting any cats on walls in case it makes him grumpier.

'I don't care about similes!' he roars back. 'I care about having some peace and quiet to enjoy my garden!'

'Sorry,' says Polly quietly. 'If you could please

just throw our Frisbee back, we'll try to be a bit quieter.'

'You'd better be!' the Really Grumpy Man shouts back. 'And you can forget about your Frisbee until you can learn some manners! Now, stop your racket and BE QUIET!'

He disappears back behind his fence and Polly and I just stare at each other. Who is this grumpy man? Where is Elsie? And who said anything about racquets – we haven't played tennis since we hit all the balls up on the garage roof?

We look at the throw-and-catch ball, but decide against it. We don't want the Really Grumpy Man to shout at us again, and throw and catch isn't as much fun without the laughing and the squealing. In fact, nothing is as much fun without the laughing and the squealing, so we go inside instead.

In the kitchen, Dad and Rita are cooking dinner

together. Dad and Rita do everything together (*except for going to the toilet, by the way. I hope.*) and they laugh and squeal a lot, so they must be having fun too. Rita is cooking something yummy and gives Dad a spoonful.

'Oh, my days – that's the most delicious thing I've ever tasted!' he beams (*he says that about every single thing that Rita cooks, by the way, even when she just puts cereal in a bowl*). He gives her a great big kiss and hugs her while she stirs her cooking. They are playing some old people's music from the 1990s, which is fine because it makes them happy and Polly and I can put on our UniMingo playlist after tea.

'What are you two doing in here?' Rita smiles. 'It's a beautiful evening – go and enjoy the sunshine.'

'We can't,' Polly grumbles, slumping down at the kitchen table.

'Why not?' Dad asks, kissing Rita again, who

giggles. They are so cute. Gross, but cute.

'There's a Really Grumpy Man out there,' I explain.

'What?' says Dad, dropping Rita, who drops her spoon. 'Where?'

'Over the fence,' I tell him. 'Elsie's fence.'

'Ohhhh,' says Dad, looking relieved and hugging Rita again. 'That must be Barry. He's our new neighbour.'

'What new neighbour?' I ask. 'Where's Elsie?'

'Oh, sweetie,' says Dad, coming over and kissing my head. 'Elsie had to move out. She's gone to a home.'

'Well, that's just silly,' I point out. 'She had a perfectly good home next door to us.'

'A retirement home,' Rita explains. 'She was a very old lady and the house was getting too much for her.'

'She wasn't that old,' I remark. 'She was like – fifty-four?'

'Sweetie, she was eighty-seven,' Dad says.

Oh. Close enough.

'So who is this Grumpy Barry?' says Polly, sounding almost as grumpy as Grumpy Barry.

'We don't call people names,' says Rita in a Mum way.

'Okay – who is this Barry? Who is very grumpy,' Polly says with a sweet grin. I try not to laugh. I think Rita and Dad are trying not to laugh too.

'He is our new neighbour – he moved in yesterday with his wife, Sheila,' Dad explains.

'Well, he just shouted at us,' Polly grumbles.

'Well, maybe you need to be more careful about your noise levels,' Rita says.

'Elsie didn't mind the noise levels,' I say.

'Elsie had a hearing aid,' Dad says. 'And I don't think she always had it switched on. Do you remember the time we had to go round to tell her that her TV was blasting at full volume? At four a.m.? On the Weather Channel?'

Hmmm. That might also explain why Elsie always called me Charlotte.

'We all have to live together,' says Dad, going back to cuddling Rita. 'So let's all try to get along. I'm sure Barry is a very reasonable man.'

Polly and I look at each other. Grumpy Barry seems about as reasonable as a … really unreasonable person (*not sure if that counts as a simile, by the way, but it's true*).

Grumpy Barry is a meanie.

Just ask my pink Frisbee.

CHAPTER 12 – 8

'*Stinky Scarlett smells of stink! What will all the stinkers think? Let's be glad she's not a drink! Stinky, stinky Scarlett!*'

So like I said, William U is back at St Lidwina's.

'William, you are not making kind choices,' Maisie says to him as he sings his stupid song across the table. 'Please stop, or I will go and talk to Ms Pitt-Bull about it.'

'Ooooh – *I'll go and talk to Ms Pitt-Bull about it*,' William U says, but much more quietly.

'Sarcasm is the lowest form of wit,' Maisie replies.

'What does that even mean?' scoffs William U.

'It means "be quiet, you sound like a big twit",'

Maisie explains.

'William U!' Ms Pitt-Bull calls. 'Can you come here, please?'

Ha! William U has to go and speak to Ms Pitt-Bull. Serves him right. I try not to look too smug.

It doesn't work, but at least I tried.

William U goes over to Ms Pitt-Bull, who starts talking to him quietly. Maisie and I go back to our work. It's writing time and we're trying to write an acrostic poem, which is when you put a word down the side and have to make a poem out of the letters going across. We're using our names, which is a bit unfair, because I've got eight letters in my name and I'm stuck on the second T. Sam on the Blue Table for Literacy finished ages ago.

'There has to be a way,' I say quietly to Maisie. 'You can't leave.'

'I know,' says Maisie. 'But what choice do I have?'

We're talking (*again*) about Maisie's foster family leaving (*again*) and her having to find a new foster family (*again*).

'I've got about as much chance of staying at St Lidwina's as our next head teacher,' Maisie sighs, using a very good simile that I'm sure would get her a sparkly sticker if she wrote it down. 'But all my foster families have been really nice. I'm sure the next one will be too.'

'But they might not be near here,' I say. 'And you're my School BFF.'

We sit and look at each other with sad eyes. I can feel The Crying trying to come up my throat again, but I swallow it down with spit.

'I brought my new UniMingo skipping rope I got for my birthday,' Maisie says more brightly. 'We can play with it at break time. It'll be fun.'

'Maybe,' I smile back. I'm still not sure about having fun without my granny. And I'm still trying not to think about who I will play with at break time if Maisie leaves as it makes The Crying try to start again.

I look over at Karam's acrostic poem. It's really good – and he's got a K in his name, which is tricky to find words for. Just ask Kendrick.

'Scarlett?' Ms Pitt-Bull calls across the classroom as William U comes and sits down quietly without saying anything mean (*which is weird, by the way*). 'Could you come here, please?'

Uh-oh. I'm in trouble for talking (*again*).

I put down my pencil (*I haven't got my pen licence yet, which I don't mind, by the way, because pencil's much better and you can rub out your mistakes and not get ink all over your fingers, so I don't know what the big deal about having a pen licence is anyway*) and walk over to Ms Pitt-Bull's table.

'Yes, miss?' I ask, like I don't know what she's going to say.

'I just wanted to check in with you,' Ms Pitt-Bull smiles. 'To make sure you're okay.'

'I'm fine,' I say. This is the strangest telling-off I've ever had.

'I know that you recently suffered a bereavement,' says Ms Pitt-Bull quietly. 'And I know that can be very hard. How are you?'

'I'm fine,' I say unsurely. 'But I haven't suffered any burritos. We don't really eat Mexican food now Rita's moved in as it gives my dad really bad wind and—'

'I meant about your grandmother,' says Ms Pitt-Butt gently. 'I know you were very close. You must miss her very much.'

Oh. She's talking about Granny. I don't really know what to say.

'Grief doesn't go in a straight line,' Ms Pitt-Bull says. 'Some days you're up. Some you're down. Some days you're both. All are absolutely normal and all are absolutely fine.'

I nod. I don't really want to be talking about this. I want to figure out what else starts with T for my acrostic poem and get outside to not play with Maisie's UniMingo skipping rope.

'So if you need some time or space, or you want to talk,' Ms Pitt-Bull carries on, 'just let me know.'

I nod again and swallow hard. Ms Pitt-Bull being nice is making me feel … weird. I can feel The Crying coming up in my throat. I am NOT going to cry. Not here, not in front of the whole of Rainbow Class, not when Meanie William Meanie U will see me and be even meaner and—

'DAAAAARLINGS!'

The Crying sinks straight back down my throat as a lady with lots of curly grey hair, glasses on a chain and scarves on every bit of her body shouts from the doorway. Rainbow Class all stop what they're doing and look towards the door.

'Ah,' says Ms Pitt-Bull, suddenly sounding very tired. 'Headmistress. Do come in.'

So this is our new head teacher. Our deputy head, Ms De Promotion, has been running the school (*again*) since our last head teacher left (*again*), but this week we found out we have a new Head (*again*).

'Children,' says Ms Pitt-Bull, shaking the quiet bells. 'Come to your carpet spaces.'

We all go and sit on our carpet spaces, trying to find enough room to sit without sitting on each other's heads. There's not nearly as much space for everybody in the summer term as there was at the beginning of September. I think the carpet might be shrinking.

'Thank you, everybody,' says Ms Pitt-Bull, shaking the bells again. 'Let's give a warm Rainbow Class welcome to our new headmistress – Madame Flounce.'

We all sing our Welcome Song. We're getting very good at it because we've sung it to so many head teachers this year. Normally teachers just stand there and smile while we sing. But Madame Flounce rolls back her head, before starting to conduct us.

'Yes ... yes ... such tone ... think of your diction ... does anyone want to try the descant?'

45

she sings out over us, waving her arms around and making her scarves waft into Ms Pitt-Bull's face.

We finish the song and clap like we always do when welcoming someone new to our class. Madame Flounce steps to the side before putting a hand on her heart and doing a curtsey.

'Thank you, thank you so much,' she says, curtseying on the other side. Ms Pitt-Bull blows another bit of scarf out of her face. Madame Flounce pats her hands down, like she doesn't want us to clap any more.

'You are too, too kind,' she says. 'Firstly I'd like to thank my previous employer, The Florence Foster Jenkins Stage School, for releasing me from my role as creative director to take up this post. I'm delighted that my final production of *Starlight Express* created such a strong response. Whoever said that putting seven-year-olds on roller skates was a bad idea?'

William D puts his hand up.

'Their parents?' he suggests.

Ms Pitt-Bull snorts. Maybe there's a bit of scarf still up her nose?

'But really, I must dedicate today to you, the wonderful children of St Lidwina's, for taking me into your school and your hearts.'

We all smile. It's always nice to be thanked for something you didn't get any choice about.

'I promise you that as your head teacher – your director, if you will – I will nurture your creativity. I want to make St Lidwina's ... a Centre for the Performing Arts!'

Oh. So that's the new plan.

Let me explain something.

Everyone has a plan for St Lidwina's.

Trent wanted it to be a Centre for Excellence.

Ms Spoke wanted it to be a Centre for Personal Development.

The council wanted it to be a Shopping Centre, but my granny told me they couldn't get permission for their plan.

Maybe it would be good if someone just wanted to make St Lidwina's a Centre for Really Happy Children. But maybe that's why they haven't offered me the job.

'Your life is your own production and you are the lead player,' Madame Flounce says. 'I will build your confidence. I will help your self-expression. I will— Yes, dear?'

Felix puts his hand down to ask his question.

'Will you be here longer than three months?' he asks. 'That's the record. Rory bet me a KitKat we'll have a new head teacher by the end of term.'

Madame Flounce laughs a very big laugh for a very small thing.

'While there is an audience for me here, I shall remain on the stage,' she promises, taking a bow.

Felix looks confused. I think he just wants to know about the KitKat.

'Your first performance will be at the end of this term,' Madame Flounce continues. 'I want to find the unique performer in all of you. So at the end of this term, you will produce your own class production: *Rainbow Class Has Talent*!'

Half the class squeals with excitement. The other half groans.

'I want each of you to think about your special gift,' says Madame Flounce. 'You can sing, dance, tell a story, do a magic trick – whatever your talent is, share it with us all! Now I must exit stage left. Bravo, Rainbow Class, brav— A … a … a … achoo!'

Madame Flounce does a massive sneeze. And then another, even bigger one.

'AAAAAAAACHOOOOOOOO!'

That one blows all her scarves in Ms Pitt-Bull's face again.

'Are you quite well, Headmistress?' Ms Pitt-Bull asks, pulling a scarf out of her mouth.

'It's ... it's my allergies,' sniffs Madame Flounce, taking something out of her pocket to blow her nose. I think she thinks it's a tissue. It's actually one of her scarves. 'But that's strange; I normally only react to animal hair ...'

I look over at Mr Nibbles, running happily around his wheel. So does Madame Flounce.

'EUGH!' she shrieks. 'What is THAT?'

'That's Mr Nibbles,' Maisie explains. 'He's our class pet. We love him.'

'Well, I don't,' says Madame Flounce. 'I'm horribly allergic. The classroom is no place for animals. He'll have to go.'

There is a massive gasp from everyone in Rainbow Class. Well, everyone except for Freddie, which is why he goes on The Cloud a lot for not listening.

'I'm sorry,' Ms Pitt-Bull says, not sounding sorry at all. 'Go where?'

'Anywhere but here,' says Madame Flounce, wiping her eyes with a scarf as she walks away. 'Now I'm off to inspect the playground – I want to check the acoustics for my one-woman production of *The Marriage of Figaro* I'm planning next term. But the hamster must go. I really don't need that peculiar creature in my school, irritating me all day long.'

'I know how you feel,' mutters Ms Pitt-Bull as Madame Flounce goes outside, which surprises me as I thought she really liked Mr Nibbles. 'But Mr Nibbles will need to be somewhere over the summer holidays, so perhaps it is time we found him a new home ...'

'No! She ... you ... we ... we can't do that!' someone shouts.

Someone shouting in Rainbow Class is very unusual as we have to use our indoor voices (*unless we are asking a visitor a question, by the way, when we have to use our big voices, which seems strange as they must go away thinking we shout all day*). But what's even more unusual is who is doing the shouting.

It's Maisie.

'No!' she shouts again. 'I won't let you! You can't just take Mr Nibbles's home away from him. He loves it here! He has friends! We're his family! You … you … you can't take all that away from him!'

Maisie's red glasses usually give her perspective and she is normally very calm. But right now I don't think they are helping her.

Because right now her red glasses are full of tears.

'It's all right, Maisie,' Ms Pitt-Bull says gently, waving to Maisie to come over. 'We'll find Mr Nibbles a new home. A home where he'll be very happy with a new family.'

'But … what if he's not?' Maisie sobs. 'What if his new family aren't as nice as Rainbow Class? What if they don't love him like we do? What if—'

'No one is going to let that happen, I promise you,' says Ms Pitt-Bull, holding Maisie's hands.

I'm glad she's taking this Mr Nibbles situation so seriously. 'We need someone to make sure he goes to a good home and I can't think of anyone better than you. You can help us decide the best place for him. Perhaps we can put up some posters asking if anyone can take him in. Would you do that for Mr Nibbles?'

Maisie sniffs and wipes her eyes. She nods her head.

'Good girl,' says Ms Pitt-Bull, rubbing Maisie on the back. 'Why don't you go to the bathroom and freshen up?'

I give Maisie a big smile, but my heart is sinking. This is awful. Mr Nibbles is leaving Rainbow Class! And I *really* don't want to do *Rainbow Class Has Talent*. I don't have a special talent. I'm really good at Maths, but I don't think standing on stage doing the thirteen times table is going to be very fun.

Although I'd enjoy it.

But Polly looks like she's going to take off. She does StageStarz on Saturdays, so she's really good at singing and dancing. She has loads of talents. I wish I could borrow one, like I did her green hairband last week.

'Okay, Rainbow Class, line up to go outside for morning break,' says Ms Pitt-Bull. 'When you come back, we'll return to our name poems.'

I groan. I don't really want to do my acrostic any more. Although I'm not nearly as fed up as Bartholomew.

I look out of the window to where Madame Flounce is performing in different parts of the playground.

'*Figaro!*' she sings (*at least I think that's what you call what she's doing. I've not heard a noise like that from a human before*).

Maisie comes back from the bathroom and lines

up quietly. She'll hate *Rainbow Class Has Talent*; she really doesn't enjoy going on stage. But she looks much calmer. Her red glasses must be giving her perspective again. Perhaps she cleaned them in the bathroom.

'Are you okay?' I whisper to her as we line up.

'*Figaro … Figaro!*' Madame Flounce wails outside again.

'I just think it's unfair,' she says, wiping her eyes again. 'Mr Nibbles loves it here. He shouldn't have to move because someone else says he has to. Can

he come and live with you?'

'I wish,' I grumble. 'Mum says we can't have him, even if I'm Star of the Week, because of the babies coming. And my dad is allergic to hamsters, like Madame Flounce. But he doesn't sneeze when Mr Nibbles is around. He screams and runs out of the room. It must be a really bad allergy ... But I'll help you to find him a new home, I Pinky Promise.'

We Pinky Promise to show this is serious, because Sasha in Year 6 says it's against the law

to break a Pinky Promise. And Sasha's a sixer in Brownies, so she must know how laws work.

'*Figaro, Figaro, Figaroooo!*' comes the noise from outside again.

'And I hope you're okay about the talent show,' I say. 'I know you don't like that kind of thing.'

'Oh, that's fine,' she smiles sadly. 'I'm not worried about that.'

'Why?' I ask.

My School BFF pushes her red glasses up her nose.

'Because I probably won't be here anyway.'

I feel The Crying coming back up in my throat, so I swallow again. I don't want Maisie to go. She'll be as lost as my Frisbee over Grumpy Barry's fence. I can't imagine St Lidwina's without her. Or Mr Nibbles. And I don't have a talent. I really need some help, but the only person I really want to talk to is Granny, but I can't because I've suffered burritos and she's not here any more and I can feel The Crying getting stronger, but I don't want to start in case I never stop and the swallowing isn't working and I'm worried I'm going to—

Suddenly the playground goes really dark as a massive black storm cloud covers the blue sky. With a rumble that sounds like Grumpy Barry shouting over the fence, the cloud bursts open.

'*Figaro, Figaro, Figar-OOOOOOHHHHHHH!*' Madame Flounce screams. The cloud empties right over her head, completely soaking her and hammering down on our window. It's really funny – and it stopped the terrible singing.

But everyone still groans. It's raining. We all know what this means …

'Oh dear,' sighs Ms Pitt-Bull. 'Wet play it is. Back to your tables.'

We all stomp back to our places. Wet play is the actual worst. Instead of running and climbing and playing, we have to do jigsaws and draw stuff. I look outside. Madame Flounce is running towards the school, her scarves dripping soggily around her.

Good.

Maisie folds up her skipping rope sadly and puts it back in her tray. I look down at my acrostic poem. Now I have a word for my second 'T'.

Terrible.

Because that's what today is.

CHaPTeR √25

It's after school and I've been waiting for Aunty Amara to pick me up. I knew it would be a long wait, because Aunty Amara often forgets to pick me up. So I'm still in the classroom with Maisie, whose foster mum is stuck in traffic (*in her car; she's not just standing there*) and Karam, whose dad is running late (*although he's not running, he's in a car too – silly Unwords*). Maisie and I are drawing posters to try to find a new home for Mr Nibbles. I Find Drawing a Challenge, so I'm trying to copy what Maisie is doing. Karam is very quiet. He doesn't look very happy so I ask him if wants to join in.

'Do you want to join in?' I say, because that's

the best way to ask.

'No. Thank you,' he says quietly.

'Are you okay, Karam? You look sad,' says Maisie, who notices things even when she's not looking at them (*red glasses*).

'I'm not sad. I'm worried,' says Karam. Karam only joined Rainbow Class in the Christmas term when his family moved here, even though he didn't speak any English and couldn't ask anyone how to learn it. Arabic is Karam's first language – but now he's already BRILLIANT at speaking English too, which is really impressive because we've been learning Spanish for a year and I still can't count to eight.

One of the really good things about people who don't speak English as their first language is that they just say what they mean because they haven't learned all the silly Unwords that confuse everything. Jakub's the same – he speaks really good English, even though his first language is Polish. I think it's very helpful when he says what he means, although Mum tells him off sometimes, like when we were moving house and Mum said she needed 'a moment' and Jakub explained that meant the babies are making her fart a lot. I didn't think the removal men minded one bit, but Mum didn't see it that way and made Jakub unpack the garage all by himself.

'What are you worried about?' I ask Karam. I'm a bit of an expert at Worry Wobbles as they are one of my BIG FEELINGS. Although I can't always control them, like when I had to go and get my verruca frozen off and I made the skeleton in the nurse's office lose a foot and three ribs.

'*Rainbow Class Has Talent*,' Karam sighs. 'I can't do anything.'

'Yes, you can!' says Maisie, putting her felt tips down. 'You can name all the dinosaurs in two

languages. You're really good at football. *And* you got a sparkly sticker for knowing all the flags in Geography last week.'

'But I can't do this at the talent show,' says Karam. 'I'm going to look bad.'

I can see Maisie thinking hard. This is good, because I don't know how to help Karam so, a bit like the poster, the best thing I can do is copy her.

'What did you like doing at your old school?' Maisie asked. 'Before you moved here.'

Karam shrugged.

'I liked writing,' he said. 'I liked writing stories and poems.'

'Me too!' says Maisie.

'But my writing isn't as good in English,' says Karam sadly. 'I'm still learning and sometimes I use the wrong words.'

'We all use the wrong words sometimes,' I say. 'Until Year 2 I called balloons "baboons". When

I told everyone there were going to be loads of baboons at my seventh birthday party, they were a bit disappointed that the village hall wasn't full of monkeys.'

Karam laughs.

'But we can help you,' I tell him, because I think we can. 'You've got loads of good ideas, Maisie is really good at writing and I'm really good at talking. I know that because every time I talk in the middle of class, Ms Pitt-Bull says, "Thank you, Scarlett."'

'If you tell us your ideas, we can help you to write them down – but only if you want us to,' says Maisie. 'I'm sure you can do it without us; you're really clever. You probably just need some confidence.'

'This is a big help!' says Karam, a big smile now on his face. 'Perhaps we can start now?'

'Sure,' says Maisie. 'My foster mum will be ages

– the traffic on the A627 is a nightmare at this time. I keep telling her to take the bypass.'

'And the office will need to phone my aunty,' I say. 'And my aunty will need to find her phone, so …'

'Great!' says Karam. 'And perhaps I can help you with your posters?'

'Please,' I say, because I really do need some help. Karam is good at drawing. And my Mr Nibbles looks like a hairy baked bean.

'Then let's get started,' Maisie smiles. She's such a good friend – to everyone, not just me. I feel The Crying coming up in my throat, but I swallow it down. Because I don't want to think about it.

I don't want to think what we're all going to do without her.

When Aunty Amara finally finds her phone and then finally finds me, she takes me to her

Over-Sixties art therapy group, even though I'm not Over-Sixty, but Aunty Amara says they'll 'make an exception' (*which means 'completely break the rules' – silly Unwords*). I can't go straight home because Mum and Jakub have an appointment to 'check on the babies', which I think is a bit pointless because the babies are very obviously there – Mum can't even see her own feet, her tummy is so big now.

But everything is fun with Aunty Amara, so I'm happy that we are going to the library to meet her group. Even if we are twenty-five minutes late.

When we arrive, there are lots of Actual Over-Sixties drawing a pineapple.

'Hi, everyone. Sorry I'm late, couldn't find my new glasses anywhere – they were in my sock drawer,' says Aunty Amara. 'This is my gorgeous niece Scarlett, who'll be joining us today. Scarlett, why don't you go and sit over there, next to Sadie?'

Aunty Amara gives me a piece of paper and points to an empty stool. I walk over and put my paper on the easel (*which I now know is the board where you put your drawing paper, by the way, and not the same as a 'weasel', which is a big furry rat thing that you probably don't want to draw on*) and start to draw my pineapple. I look at it and I try to draw what's there. But whenever I draw, something gets a bit lost between my eyes and my hands, because the pineapple on my paper looks nothing like the pineapple on the table.

'That's lovely,' says the Over-Sixty next to me, who must be Sadie because Aunty Amara said she was and she wouldn't fib about something like that.

'Thank you,' I say. I look at my pineapple. It looks like a melted igloo. I *really* Find Drawing a Challenge.

But Sadie is *really* good. 'Yours actually looks like an actual pineapple.'

'You're very kind,' says Sadie. 'It's so nice to meet you, Scarlett. Your aunty has told us so much about you. She's very proud.'

'Of my drawing?' I say, looking back at my melted igloo. 'Really?'

'Of you,' smiles Sadie, putting the finishing touches to her Actual Pineapple. 'Family is a wonderful thing. You must cherish each other.'

'Are your family good at drawing pineapples?' I ask her, because Granny always said it was polite to ask people about themselves. Sadie laughs.

'My sister Flora got most of the artistic talent,' says Sadie. 'She's the one who encouraged me to join this group.'

'Which Over-Sixty is she?' I ask, looking around the room.

Sadie makes a sad smile.

'Flora passed away six months ago,' she says quietly.

Oh. That's sad. Passed Away is a Polite Olden Days way of saying that someone died.

'That's really sad,' I say, because it is.

'Yes, it is,' she says, sniffing in a sad way. 'We were best friends – we did everything together. When I lost her ... Well, I felt like I lost a piece of me.'

'My granny di— passed away too,' I tell Sadie, feeling The Crying coming up my throat. 'I don't feel like I've lost a piece of me exactly – I don't think Granny would have fitted inside me, she was quite tall. But there's a big ... space where she should be.'

Sadie smiles again.

'That's a very clever way of explaining it,' she says. 'I feel a big space where Flora should be. When she died, I stopped doing all the things we used to do together. I didn't like the big space next to me.'

'I understand that,' I say. 'Since Granny died, I feel like I shouldn't really have fun. Like it's … rude or something.'

'Yes!' says Sadie. 'That's exactly how it feels! But do you think your granny would think it was rude of you to have fun?'

I think about this for a minute.

'No,' I realise. 'She really wouldn't. Granny loved fun. So long as it was polite fun. And fun that wiped its feet on the mat afterwards.'

'She sounds like a very lovely lady,' says Sadie. 'And I know that Flora wouldn't want me to stop having fun either. I took a bit of persuading from your Aunty Amara. But eventually I did come back to the group. And I'm very glad I did. I have lots of friends here, who made me feel better. A lot of us here have lost loved ones. That can be very lonely. So it's a special place for us all to come together and do something we love. And now we're all friends, people go out for meals together, even holidays. It's a very special place.'

Sadie waves at her Over-Sixty friends, who wave back.

'And you get to draw really good pineapples,' I point out.

'And you get to draw really good pineapples,' Sadie repeats with a smile, although I'm not sure why because I literally just said that.

'Sadie!' cries Aunty Amara, coming over to us and clapping her hands. 'That's just wonderful! And, Scarlett! You're so … creative!'

I laugh a bit. Aunty Amara would never tell me my drawing is rubbish, even though we both know it is.

Sadie and I carry on chatting and drawing. It's a nice thing to do. I can see why Sadie likes it here.

It's just a shame I'll have to wait until I'm Over-Sixty to join the group.

'Hey, pickle!' booms Jakub's big voice across the room a bit later. 'Hi, everyone!'

All the Over-Sixties smile and wave at Jakub. He comes over and looks at my picture.

'Wow!' he says. 'That's such a brilliant rabbit!'

I laugh. Jakub is so funny. Especially when he looks a bit confused like he does now.

'Come on, monkey,' he says, picking up my school bag. 'Mum's in the car. Time to go home for tea.'

'It was lovely talking to you, Scarlett,' says Sadie.

'You too, Sadie,' I smile back at her. 'I bet your sister was really nice, because you're really nice and sisters are often a bit the same. Except for Keisha and Lily-Mac in Year 4 who are non-identical twins and one really likes peanut butter and the other hates frogs.'

'Well, that's a very kind thing to say,' says Sadie, who looks like she might be keeping The Crying in too. 'I very much hope we meet again.'

'Oh, we will,' I say. 'Mum and Jakub are always getting Aunty Amara to look after me when they're busy, or tired, or just a little bit can't be bothered, so I'll see you soon probably.'

'I look forward to it,' says Sadie, and I wave to Aunty Amara as Jakub picks me up and piggybacks me out to the car.

'Did you have fun?' Mum asks as I get my seatbelt on in the back. I think of Granny and how she would want me to have not-rude fun.

'Yes,' I say, showing her my picture. 'Yes, I really did.'

'Oh, Scarlett,' says Mum, starting to cry again. 'What a lovely picture of me ...'

ChapTeR 2 + 8 - 4

Today is Saturday and I am at my new house. Although I was sad to leave our old house, our new house at Tottington Hall is SUPER good. It's REALLY big, with five bedrooms, a kitchen we can eat in, a dining room we can eat in if we don't want to eat in the kitchen, two living rooms (*one is my playroom, but I can still eat in it if I want*) and loads of toilets, which we don't use for eating at all. We've got our own big garden and Jakub is going to build me a treehouse in the big oak tree at the bottom, which he's *extremely* excited about because it means playdates and sleepovers in the garden and I think one day I might be allowed those things too.

Because she's got two babies in her massive tummy and Jakub has a job that gives him more money and we have a free house now, Mum took a break from being an engineer and building things for other people so she can rest before the babies come. But all that's happened is that now she's getting other people to build things on our house, which is weird because it's already much bigger than our old house and we all fitted in that one just fine. At the moment it's the conservatory, which is supposed to be a pretty glass building on the back of the house, but right now is just a big hole in the dining room.

'No, the conservatory needs to be finished THIS WEEK!' she shouts down the phone at the builders (*she Shouts At The Builders A LOT, by the way. I think it might be why they're on the phone and not here*). 'I need everything ready for when the twins come! I can't very well have two babies in a house that doesn't have a back wall!'

 78

Personally, I don't think the babies will mind that much, but I've learned not to get involved when Mum is Shouting At The Builders.

I'm in my room unpacking boxes – I've only had six weeks to do it, so I'm not finished yet – when I find Granny's Memory Book in the drawer I keep all my rubbers and sequins in. I pick it up and smell it again – it smells of Granny's house and I feel The Crying in my throat again ...

But I am NOT going to cry.

'Come along – chop, chop!' Granny would have said. 'No time like the present.' (*I don't know why time doesn't like presents, by the way. I think they're brilliant.*)

I know Granny wanted me to do this job for her, so I need to get the Memory Book done. I pick up the book and walk downstairs. I'll start with Mum. She must have a lovely memory for Granny's book.

'... NO, I SAID "ESSENCE OF EGG SHELL" FOR THE LOUNGE!!' she Shouts At The Builders. 'WHY WOULD I WANT TO PAINT MY BIGGEST ROOM IN A COLOUR CALLED "DEAD SALMON"?!'

Perhaps I'll start with Jakub instead.

The bad side of Jakub's job is that he has to do it all the time. The good side is that Jakub's job is just outside our house, so when I'm at home I get to see him loads. Being Lady Tottington-Snoot's groundskeeper is a big job, so when I'm not too busy I help him by going to talk to him.

I put the Memory Book in my backpack and walk outside our house, through our little gate and into the big, green grounds of Tottington Hall. It's been really fun exploring. When Polly comes over we go into the woods, or through the hedge maze (*which we always get lost in and Jakub has to come and rescue us, which gives him a nice break from doing his job*) or play chase on the huge lawn. We have to be a bit careful, because Lady Tottington-Snoot, who owns the massive house and all this garden, thinks that children should be seen and not heard. But luckily, as Tottington Hall is so huge and Lady Tottington-Snoot can't see or hear all that well, we can be not seen and not heard quite easily, which probably works best for us all.

I find Jakub in the rose garden, which always smells really nice, unless Jakub is putting manure (*which is animal poo, by the way*) all over the ground. There are roses of all colours – red, pink, yellow, orange, white. I think it's his favourite bit

of the whole garden, even though it hasn't got a slide in it like ours has. He's on one knee, cutting some straggly bits off the bushes to make them look neat, which is funny because Jakub has loads of straggly bits and he never cuts them off to look neat at all.

'Is Mum okay? Are the babies On Their Way?' he asks anxiously as I walk up, dropping the cutters on the floor and looking like he's getting ready to run. Jakub is convinced that the babies are On Their Way any second, even though there is another six weeks before they are due to arrive. And given that Mum is always late for everything, I expect the babies will take after her and be late too. Every time I come and see Jakub at the moment, he thinks I've come to tell him that the babies are On Their Way. I understand why he's worried. I've learned a bit more about how babies are born and they don't have very far to go so it can't take that long. But Jakub's not been a biological daddy before, so I think we're all going to have to help him through this together.

'She's fine,' I grin at him. 'She's Shouting At The Builders.'

'Oh – phew,' says Jakub, picking up his cutters. 'That's okay then. I'll just finish these, then come home and get started on our treehouse.'

'You mean *my* treehouse?' I point out.

'That's what I said,' grins Jakub, waggling his eyebrows.

'Jakub?' I ask him, sitting on the grass next to him. 'Do you have—'

'James!' comes Lady Tottington-Snoot's voice over the hedge. 'James! Where are you?'

(By the way, Lady Tottington-Snoot calls Jakub 'James' because she says she can't pronounce his name. I do not understand this. You say his name 'Ya-kub'. You say her name 'Lay-dee-Tot-ing-ten-snoot'. Hers is much harder to say.)

'Uh … here! I'm here, Your Ladyship!' Jakub burbles, jumping to his feet like the babies are actually On Their Way. 'Here I am!'

'Have you seen Boris?' she demands. 'I haven't seen him since I told him off for doing a Number Two on the floor and leaving it for someone else to clean it up! I don't have time for such matters! It took me at least ten minutes to find someone else to clean it up!'

(*Boris is one of Lady Tottington-Snoot's cats, by the way. He's not a person who left some manure*

on the floor. Lady Tottington-Snoot has loads of cats – Teresa, David, Margaret, Winston – she's always going on about how individual they all are, but they all just seem to sit around making a mess and waiting for someone else to clean up after them.)

'I'm afraid not, Your Ladyship,' Jakub stammers – Lady Tottington-Snoot makes him very nervous. 'Would you like me to help you look for him?'

'No,' sighs Lady Tottington-Snoot. 'You still have the hedges and the herbaceous borders to do when you're finished there.'

'As you wish,' says Jakub sadly. I don't think he's going to start *my* treehouse today after all.

Lady Tottington-Snoot bustles off, shouting for Boris as she goes. I expect he's hiding somewhere with the lady cat from the housekeeper's cottage – that one always has a new girlfriend. I wait for Jakub to start his cutting again, before pulling the Memory Book out of my backpack.

'Jakub?' I ask again. 'Do you have a special memory of Granny?'

Jakub smiles.

'I have many special memories of your granny,' he says. 'She was a very memorable lady. Very formidable.'

I smile. Jakub was even more scared of my granny than he is of Lady Tottington-Snoot.

'But if you had to pick just one?' I ask him.

Jakub stops cutting and has a think. A big grin spreads across his face.

'When I told her I was going to ask your mum to marry me,' he grins, 'she made me sign a contract.'

'A contract?' I ask.

'Yes,' Jakub laughs. 'She wrote it down right in front of me. She wrote a contract on a piece of paper saying that I promised I would always make your mum happy. She wouldn't give us her blessing until I signed it.'

'Did you?'

'Of course!' Jakub says. 'All I have ever wanted is to make your mum happy. And I thought it was rather wonderful that Nancy insisted upon it. I still have it in a box somewhere.'

'Can I have it?' I ask him. 'I'm making this Memory Book. Granny asked me to.'

'Did she now?' Jakub smiles. 'This is a wonderful idea. Of course I'll find it for you to put in your book. When my *dziadek* – my grandfather – died, I kept a pot that he used to keep his pipe tobacco in. For years, I'd open the pot and it would remind me of sitting on his lap while he smoked his pipe. It was a great comfort; made him feel close. Even if the pipe smoke was disgusting and always made me cough.'

I hold the book to my nose and smell it again. It smells a little bit of Granny. That makes me feel sort of happy, sort of sad. I don't know if it's a comfort. But I don't want to stop smelling it.

'Can you tell Mum that I'm going to be late for dinner?' Jakub sighs.

'Sure,' I say, jumping to my feet. 'I'll tell her while she's still Shouting At The Builders – that way she'll be all shouted out by the time you come home late again.'

'Great idea, squidge,' says Jakub, putting a muddy finger on my nose. 'See you later.'

'See ya,' I say, skipping out of the rose garden back towards home. I'm glad I've got the first thing for my Memory Book. Granny will be … would have been … really pleased with me.

The thought that I can't show Granny what I've done brings The Crying back to my throat. I try to swallow, but I haven't had a drink for ages, so I don't have enough spit to push it down. It starts to get darker and I can see a black storm cloud starting to drift across the sky.

'Miaow!'

I stop and look around. That was a cat. And not a very happy cat.

'Miiiiiaaaaaaaaow!'

I look above me. The black cloud is breaking up, but in the tree above my head is a big ball of yellow fluff.

'Boris?!' I say. 'How did you get up there?'

Boris doesn't reply. I didn't really expect him to. But he looks like he doesn't know how to get back down again.

'Don't worry,' I tell him. 'I'll come and get you.'

Luckily for Boris, I am SUPER good at climbing up trees. Just ask Jakub – he's come to get me back down from loads of them.

This is a good climbing tree – I've been up it lots of times – so I put my feet on the lower branches and start to climb towards the trembling Boris.

'It's okay,' I tell him. 'I'm an expert at getting stuck in trees. I'll get you down again.'

I reach the branch he's sitting on – it's nice and big, so I can sit with my legs either side of it. I pull myself along until I reach him.

'Miiiiiiiiiiiiaaaaaaaaaaaaaaaooooooooooooow!' he squeals. He's really scared.

'Hi, Boris,' I say as kindly as I can, so he knows I'm his friend. 'I'm Scarlett. I'm here to help you.'

I hold out my hand. Boris looks like he's not

sure, but eventually puts his little cat nose on it. It tickles and I laugh.

'Now,' I say, reaching out for him. 'I'm going to need you to come here. Come on … it's okay …'

Boris has a bit of a think about it. He looks down and realises it's quite a long way down. And he's smelled me (*lucky Jakub hadn't put manure on the roses*) and seems to think I'm okay. So with a shaking paw he starts to walk towards me.

'That's it,' I say. 'Well done, you're doing really well!'

He takes gentle, slow steps towards me, until I can reach out and pick him up. I give him a big cuddle and he purrs a bit.

'You see!' I tell him. 'It's not so bad. Now. To get you down I'm going to need both my hands. So you need to get in here.'

I put him carefully on the branch and take my backpack off. He looks at it. I don't think he's very impressed.

'Oh – I know!' I say, an idea suddenly coming into my head. 'You might like this.'

I pull out the rest of yesterday's ham sandwich and take out the ham. I put it inside the bag and Boris walks gently towards it. I hold the bag wide open so he can get in comfortably, then I turn him round so I can put the bag back on my back.

'There you go, it's okay,' I say, as I put my backpack on my shoulders, with Boris's head sticking out of the top. I reverse back along the branch and find the smaller branches to put my feet on. It's a bit harder with a cat on your back, but slowly and carefully we find our way back to the ground.

'Well done!' I say as we reach the ground and I take him out of the bag. 'You did it!'

I give Boris a squeeze, just as a slow clapping starts up nearby.

'Well, I must say, young lady – that was very impressive.'

I turn round.

There is Lady Tottington-Snoot.

'Er … thanks,' I say, not sure if I'm allowed to be seen or heard. She holds out her arms and I give her Boris.

'You are very naughty!' says Lady Tottington-Snoot sternly. 'What were you thinking, climbing that tree, you little scamp?!'

'I'm sorry, I was just trying to—'

'Not you!' she says. 'The cat!' She gives him a

long, hard stare. Boris settles into her arms and looks like he a) doesn't care, and b) is going to fall asleep anyway. It's been a long day for him. He must be tired.

'What's your name?' she says.

'Um … Boris?' I remind her.

'Not the cat!' she says. 'You!'

'Oh,' I reply. 'I'm Scarlett. Scarlett Fife.'

'Well, Miss Fife, I would like to thank you for rescuing my naughty Boris. You are to come to tea next week.'

'O… kay,' I say. I'm not sure if it's an invitation or an instruction.

'Thursday,' she says, turning round. 'Four p.m. And don't be late. I can't abide lateness.'

She heads back towards her house and I head back towards mine. Tea with Lady Tottington-Snoot? Mum will be so happy …

'… AND IF YOU TELL ME THERE ARE

GOING TO BE ANY MORE DELAYS TO THIS BUILD, I WILL COME OVER THERE AND PERSONALLY KICK YOUR BACKSIDE INTO THE MIDDLE OF NEXT WEEK ...'

Or maybe not.

I leave Mum Shouting At The Builders in the kitchen and go to the front room, where Aunty Rosa and Aunty Amara are whispering.

'I know you're stressed, but the sooner we get past this last meeting, the sooner it will be official,' Aunty Amara says. 'I just want to know this is final.'

'Everything is on track,' says Aunty Rosa. She sounds tired. 'We're so nearly there. Once it's all approved next week, at least we can start telling everyone ...'

'Tell us what?' I ask, coming into the room. Aunty Rosa quickly shuffles some papers together

and stuffs them in her work bag.

'Nothing, squidge,' she says with a Not-Very-Real smile. 'Just some boring grown-up stuff.'

My heart feels a bit heavy. That's the sort of thing Mum and Dad used to say when they got their divorce.

'But what were you—' I begin, but Aunty Amara interrupts.

'What have you been up to?' she says with another Not-Very-Real smile. 'You're covered in leaves – you look like a bird's nest!'

'I've been rescuing Boris,' I tell her.

Aunty Amara and Aunty Rosa look at each other.

'Is Boris okay?' they ask.

'He's fine,' I tell them. 'He was a bit worried at first, but once I gave him some leftover ham sandwich, he calmed down.'

'Okay,' says Aunty Rosa slowly as Mum walks into the room.

'Can you BELIEVE it?!' she says as Aunty Amara gets up to help her sit in the chair (*my mum is so big with the twins now that she needs help to sit down and stand up*). 'The builders are now saying it will be TWO WEEKS before they can get back and finish the conservatory! TWO WEEKS! I could build it myself by the weekend! In fact, I might just—'

'NO!' say Aunty Rosa and Aunty Amara together.

I think of the Memory Book in my bag. Maybe this would be a good time to ask everyone for memories of Granny.

'So, Emi – I'm going to Mum's next week. To clear the house,' says Aunty Rosa. 'The estate agent wants to put it up for sale as soon as possible.'

I feel The Crying come up in my throat. I know Granny doesn't need her house any more. But I sort of hoped we might keep it. I thought we could use it to remember her, just like the souvenir dolphin I got from SeaLand.

'Okay, I'll come and help you,' yawns Mum (*the babies also make her very tired now, by the way. As does Shouting At The Builders*).

'Don't be silly,' snaps Aunty Rosa. 'You need to get your feet up.'

'I'm fine,' yawns Mum again. 'I'll be there. How are you going with your … What was it you're doing again, Amara?' (*The babies also make Mum very forgetful. Just this week, she's nearly walked out of the supermarket without paying for her shopping, left the bath running and nearly flooded our new house and completely forgot to buy me the CD of* UniMingoes 3: 50 Songs To Live In Your Heart and Your Ears For Ever.)

'My Over-Sixties art therapy group,' Aunty Amara reminds her. 'Not well, I'm afraid. The library closes next week and I still don't have anywhere new to go. We need somewhere really big and light – I just can't find anywhere that would work. If I can't find a new venue, we'll have to stop the group, which would be so sad.'

'What?' I say, even though I heard exactly what she said. 'You can't stop the group! Sadie and her friends need it! It's where all the Over-Sixties make friends and draw pineapples!'

'I know, my darling girl,' says Aunty Amara. 'But if I can't find us somewhere new, I'll have no choice.'

'Well, I'm going to find you somewhere to have your group,' I say, and I really mean it. 'Sadie and the other Over-Sixties just need a new home. Like Mr Nibbles.'

'Where's Mr Nibbles going?' Aunty Rosa asks.

'Our new headmistress says he has to leave because she's allergic,' I explain. 'Perhaps you could have him in your Big Posh House?! You've got loads of room! Pllleeeeeaaaaase?' (*I added that bit because it always works on my aunties.*)

Aunty Rosa and Aunty Amara look at each other in a strange way.

'I'm sorry, squidge,' Aunty Rosa says. 'Now's not the best time. There's a lot going on right now.'

I knew it. They can't have Mr Nibbles because they're getting divorced and won't have their Big Posh House any more that can fit two lounges and a hamster. This isn't fair. I can feel The Crying. So I try to think about something else. Granny's Memory Book. That's a nice thing to think about.

'Er, Mum, Aunty Rosa ... if you're going to Granny's house, perhaps you could get something for my—' I start, but then both Mum's and Aunty Rosa's phones ring.

'Hello!' they both snap at the same time.

'No!' Aunty Rosa roars as she storms out of the front room. 'Any further delay is TOTALLY unacceptable!'

'No!' Mum roars as she waddles out of the front room. 'Any further delay is TOTALLY unacceptable!'

Aunty Amara and I look at each other. And then we laugh.

'What were you trying to say?' she asks me. (*Aunty Amara always notices when I'm trying to talk and the adults don't let me, by the way, and that's one of the reasons she's brilliant and I actually go to sleep when she asks me to when I stay over at their house, even if it's only midnight.*)

'So, Granny left me ... a job,' I tell her. 'She asked me to create a Memory Book for her.'

Aunty Amara smiles.

'What a wonderful idea,' she says. 'Memories are so important when we've lost someone we love.'

'Anyway,' I say, feeling The Crying come up again (*there's something about the way Aunty Amara is looking at me that makes me want to cry*). 'I wondered if you had a memory of Granny that I could put in the book?'

Aunty Amara leans back in her chair, closes her eyes and a big smile spreads across her face.

'I have so many wonderful memories of Nancy,' she says. 'She was always very kind to me. But there is one thing that really sticks in my mind – something I think would be lovely for your book.'

'Great!' I say. 'What is it?'

'Hey, everyone,' says Jakub, coming into the house looking all mucky. 'Right – I'm going to get started on that treehouse while the weather's still nice!'

He looks really tired. But I know how much he wants the treehouse, so I'm glad he's finding time for it. I look back at Aunty Amara, who is still smiling in her chair.

'A few years ago, your granny went travelling – do you remember?'

I nod. I really do. Granny decided it was time to 'broaden her horizons', which basically meant I got loads of sweets from other countries.

'Well, on her travels she visited the town in India where my parents lived before they moved to England, long before I was born. She sent me a postcard from there, saying how she understood that I had come from such a beautiful place, it explained why I was such a beautiful person ...'

Aunty Amara stops talking. The Crying has come out of her throat and is now falling down her face. I feel like mine wants to join in. But I am NOT going to cry ...

'It was a lovely thought and I kept the postcard, wondering what I should do with it,' Aunty Amara continues. 'This is the perfect place for it.'

'Thank you,' I say. I think Granny would like that memory very much. And that makes The Crying come up harder and I haven't got enough spit to swallow it down and I'm worried that The Crying is going to come out now, so I need to keep it inside and—

KER-BOOM!!!

A huge thunderclap roars outside and rain suddenly starts pouring down on the windows from the black storm cloud up above.

'I love nature,' says Aunty Amara, jumping up to the window to look at the rain. 'One minute she's all sunny, and the next she's watering the plants. How lucky we are.'

Some squelchy footprints squelch across the hallway. It's Jakub. He's absolutely drenched. I don't think he's loving nature, nor feeling very lucky.

'I'm going to have a shower,' he says quietly.

Poor Jakub.

At this rate, he's never going to get his treehouse.

CHaPTeR 14 ÷ 2

Rainbow Class Has Talent is going to take place in the school marquee on the playing field. This is because Madame Flounce is refurbishing the school hall to help make it a Centre for the Performing Arts (*which means the stage is getting curtains*). Today we are rehearsing in the big marquee. It's a warm, sunny day, which can make the marquee really hot, but luckily it's full of holes, so there's some fresh air coming in.

'PrrrrrrroJECT!' Madame Flounce is shouting at Polly as she sings her song. 'Imagine you are singing to someone right at the back of marquee.'

Polly looks confused. She *is* singing to us all at the back of the marquee – we've all been told to sit there as the big pole that holds the roof up is quite bendy and Ms Pitt-Bull said it's better to be safe than sorry, although she's quite busy filling in her form for the nice Health and Safety people.

I look around our school marquee. There are big holes, small holes, holes that have tape over them, holes where the tape has fallen off them and holes that are just deciding whether they are going to be big or small and if they need tape.

'Scarlett!' Madame Flounce calls. 'Your turn. What is your talent going to be?'

I look at the floor.

'I haven't got one,' I say quietly.

'Scarlett! PrrrrroJECT!' Madame Flounce roars. 'Imagine you are speaking to a room full of people!'

I look around. I *am* speaking to a room full of people.

'I ... I don't have one!' I call more loudly.

'Pish and nonsense!' Madame Flounce declares. 'Everyone has a talent! You just need to find something you love! Something you care about! Something you want to share with the whole world!'

She spins around on the spot, but gets tangled up in her own scarves and stumbles. She grabs on to the marquee pole for support and the whole tent wobbles. Everyone gasps.

'Don't be alarmed – I am fine!' says Madame Flounce, brushing a scarf off her head. 'The show must go on! Karam! You're next!'

'I'm not ready yet, miss,' says Karam, who is sitting in a corner with Maisie, working on his poem. It turned out that I was much better at talking than writing, so they went to find somewhere a bit quieter to write it all down. 'But nearly …'

'Where is the professionalism?' mutters Madame Flounce. 'Felix! Time for your juggling act!'

Felix heads up to the stage, carrying a box of tomatoes. Felix is really good at juggling. He does it in class with pens and pencils and scissors – although Ms Pitt-Bull drew the line when he tried to use Mr Nibbles, even though he doesn't ever drop anything and he'd put the scissors down.

I feel the Worry Wobbles in my tummy. I still haven't got a talent – what if I can't think of something to do? What if I think of something stupid and everyone laughs? What if that makes me want to cry and the whole marquee falls down in the rain? What if … ?

Oh no.

The Worry Wobbles are starting.

I watch as the pole holding the roof up starts to shake. I try to concentrate on Felix juggling his tomatoes. But the worries keep on coming. I remember what I have to do to help my Worry Wobbles – it's been working really well. I start with listing five things I can see. But the first thing I can see is a big marquee that feels like it's going to fall down on us, so that doesn't really help.

If I get angry, or worried, or upset, I don't think the marquee is going to be able to take it. Actually, I think if someone sneezes, the marquee won't be able to take it. What if my BIG FEELINGS come out on the night of *Rainbow Class Has Talent*? What if I ruin it for everyone? What if … ?

I stare and stare at Felix and his juggling tomatoes. The marquee is still wobbling, which is making the stage wobble. Felix is trying to keep control of his tomatoes, but the wobbly stage and everyone starting to make A Bit Scared noises is putting him off.

'Okay, children,' says Ms Pitt-Bull, looking nervously up at the ceiling. 'Stand up, please – calmly and quietly. I'd like you to follow me out to the playground. Now.'

We all stand up – not very calmly or quietly – and start walking out of the marquee.

'Er ... miss?' Felix says, still trying to juggle his tomatoes on the wobbly stage. 'What about me?'

'Don't let anything distract you, Felix!' says Madame Flounce. 'A great performer can carry on through any distraction!'

The Worry Wobbles are getting worse. I start playing my alphabet game to make them go away. A is for ... Aunties (*what if they get divorced?*), B is for ... Builders (*what if they never finish our house?*), C is for ... Crying (*I am NOT going to cry ...*).

This really isn't working today.

'Felix!' Ms Pitt-Bull calls to the stage. 'You come along too. I'd like everyone outside. Immediately.'

'Oh. Okay,' says Felix, and throws his tomatoes up into the air (*Felix is very good at juggling but gets quite easily distracted. Just ask the dinner ladies when he juggled everyone's yoghurts just before the bell went for lunchtime play*). He jumps off the stage and runs to join us.

'Wait!' Madame Flounce cries after him. 'It'll be all right ... on (*splat*) ... the (*splat*) ... night (*splat*)!'

Madame Flounce stops, puts a hand to her head and feels the three tomatoes that have just splatted all over her head. That makes me giggle – which always makes the Worry Wobbles calm down.

Getting outside into the fresh air also makes me feel much better and the Wobbles start to go. Maybe everything will be okay after all. I look back at the marquee. It's still standing. Phew. I *can* control my **BIG FEELINGS**. I *will* control my **BIG FEELINGS**. Granny had **BIG FEELINGS** too and she told me that I shouldn't push them down, I need to deal with them. It was really good advice and it's helped me a lot.

I'm just not going to cry.

'Children, have a play for ten minutes, then we'll start again with Vashti's origami act,' says Ms Pitt-Bull.

(*'Origami', by the way, is when you fold paper really neatly into shapes. It's not the same as 'oregano', which is what I thought it was at first and that Vashti was going to make a really nice pasta sauce for her talent. Vashti is really good at making paper into neat shapes even though she doesn't really like doing the same with her hair, which weirdly, often has pasta sauce in it.*)

'Are you okay?' Maisie asks me as we walk over

to the play trail. 'You look … Big Feeling-y.'

'I'm just a bit worried,' I tell her, because it's important to share your feelings, unless they have Bad Choice Words in them, like when Mum shares her feelings with the builders. 'What if my BIG FEELINGS spoil the show?'

'They won't,' Maisie says, pushing her glasses up her nose. 'You're getting so good at managing them now.'

'I hope so,' I say. 'What's the latest on Mr Nibbles?'

'Not good,' Maisie sighs. 'Darcy took him home, but her cats thought he was a new toy and she only just got to him in time. Emma R said her family could take him. But then she left the bath running while she filmed a dance routine on her phone and flooded her downstairs, so her mum said she wasn't responsible enough. And Rory seems very keen. But I think he really just wants to feed Mr Nibbles to his pet snake.'

Rory walks past and hisses at us with a grin.

'So I'm stuck. No one seems to want the responsibility.'

'Poor Mr Nibbles,' I say. 'That must feel horrid.'

'It must,' says Maisie quietly.

'But it's all going to be okay,' I say as we climb up to the top of the climbing frame, where we like to sit and chat. 'You've got me to help you with Mr Nibbles and I've got you to help me with my BIG FEELINGS and—'

'Yeah, Scarlett, about that …' Maisie begins, but we are interrupted by a noise underneath us, inside the climbing frame. Someone is crying.

'Who's that?' Maisie asks.

'It's probably Fleur,' I tell her. (*Fleur always cries, by the way, even when nothing's really wrong. It's why I'm glad she didn't invite me to her party, because she probably would have ended up crying all over it anyway.*)

'No – look, she's crying over there because Misha has a new hairband,' Maisie points out.

She's right. In fact, looking around the playground, I can see everyone. Everyone except …

'William!' comes a familiar voice underneath us. It's William U's mum, on playground duty. She always has to know What's Upset William. 'Oh, William! What's upset you?'

'He's probably just upset he's not Star of the

Year,' I whisper. 'Or he's got Fish-Pie-For-Lunch Aversion Syndrome. Or he's suddenly allergic to spelling tests. Or—'

'It's Daddy,' sniffs William U. 'When's he coming home?'

Oh.

So not fish pie then.

I don't look at Maisie. I know just how she'll be looking at me through her red glasses.

There's a long pause.

'William,' says William U's mum quietly. 'I told you. Daddy's not coming home. He's going to live in his new house now.'

'No!' William U shouts. 'I don't want him to live in his new house! I want him to stay with us! I want him to live in *our* house!'

We hear William U start to cry again.

'So do I, darling,' William U's mum says, sounding like she might be keeping The Crying down her throat too. 'So do I.'

Maisie and I look at each other. So William U's parents are getting a divorce? Just like my parents. Just like Aunty Rosa and Aunty Amara ...

I didn't think I could ever feel sorry for William U.

But I really, really do.

Maisie and I climb quietly down from the climbing frame and go and line up. Ms Pitt-Bull looks down the line.

'Where is William U?' Ms Pitt-Bull asks.

I put up my hand.

'He's in the climbing frame,' I say quietly. 'With his mum.'

Ms Pitt-Bull nods.

'Thank you, Scarlett. Right, Rainbow Class. Let's sit down and watch Vashti's beautiful origami.'

We all sit down on the playing field as Vashti starts making pretty paper birds and sets them

flying around the playground. She's really good. No wonder she doesn't have time to brush her hair – origami is much more fun.

'Maisie?' I ask my School BFF. 'What are you going to do for the talent show?'

Maisie looks at the grass.

'Nothing,' she whispers back.

'What?' I laugh. 'You can't stand on stage and do nothing.'

'I won't be standing on the stage,' says Maisie, pushing up her glasses. 'I won't be at *Rainbow Class Has Talent*.'

I don't understand.

'I don't understand,' I say, because I don't understand.

'Scarlett, my foster family has booked their flights. They leave next week.'

I feel The Crying start to come up my throat. I don't like this. I don't like this at all.

'So … what does that mean?' I ask her, hoping that I'm wrong about what I actually think it means.

'It means … it means I'm moving to a new family any day now,' says Maisie, looking at the floor. 'So I guess that means … I'll be leaving St Lidwina's.'

I feel The Crying race up my throat. The sky is getting darker. The cloud is coming over …

'No,' I say. 'No, you can't.'

Maisie wipes a tear from her cheek.

'Promise me we'll still be Best Forever Friends. Even when we're not at the same school?'

Vashti is throwing more paper birds around and they are flying over our heads.

I know we're supposed to sit in our own space. But I shuffle over so I can give Maisie a hug. Ms Pitt-Bull looks over at us, but she doesn't tell us off.

'We'll be Best Forever Friends wherever we are,'

I say, making a Pinky Promise with her to make it legal.

I push The Crying back down my throat. I am NOT going to cry here in front of all of Rainbow Class and Ms Pitt-Bull and Maisie and—

KER-BOOM!

The huge black storm cloud lets out a roar, before emptying its rain on to our heads. It's raining cats and dogs, like Granny used to say (*which, by the way, means it's just raining a lot, not that our playground is filled with pets*) and we're all getting wet.

'Rainbow Class!' Ms Pitt-Bull commands. 'Form an orderly line and head back to the classroom. Don't run!'

We all stand up and sprint back towards the classroom.

Just before we get there, I see one of Vashti's pretty paper birds on the ground. I pick it up and try to dry it off. But it just makes a soggy mush in my hands.

I've ruined it.

Just like I'm going to ruin *Rainbow Class Has Talent*.

But even so.

I am NOT going to cry.

ChapTeR 2 x 2 x 2

Today, Aunty Amara actually remembered to pick me and Polly up from school because Rita and my dad are both working. My dad works one day a week At The Office, which is really good because:

1) I get to see Aunty Amara

2) We get takeaway (*Aunty Amara is brilliant at everything except cooking*)

3) My dad actually brushes his hair

Now the rain has stopped, it's warm and sunny again, so Polly and I go out into the garden to play skipping. Aunty Amara came out with us at first, but now she's lost one of her shoes, so she's looking for it in the grass. (*Aunty Amara loses everything except her temper, by the way, but she's got Aunty Rosa to do that for her. Or has she now ...?*)

'Was Maisie okay today?' Aunty Amara asks. 'I saw her talking to Ms Pitt-Bull at pick-up time.'

'She was really sad,' I explain. 'She's going to have to move away.'

'Why?' asks Aunty Amara. 'She seems so settled and happy.'

'She is,' I sulk. 'But her foster family are moving to Australia and they can't find anyone in our area to give her a home. Just like Mr Nibbles – who was supposed to go home with Petra, but she has an orthodontist appointment so—'

'Say that again?' says Aunty Amara, suddenly standing very still.

'Oh. Okay,' I shrug. 'Petra has an orthodontist appointment – which means she's getting braces,

by the way, not that she's watching birds. That's called ornithology. Silly Unwords—'

'No – about Maisie,' Aunty Amara interrupts, which isn't like her, but I'm not going to make a thing of it. 'Did you say her foster family are moving away?'

'Yes,' I tell her. 'And she doesn't know where she's going to live, but she's probably going to move away from here and St Lidwina's.'

'I see,' says Aunty Amara, thinking very hard. I wait for her to say something wise and helpful. But instead she just runs into the house with her one sandal on. 'I'll be back in a minute!'

Polly and I watch her go.

'That was weird,' says Polly.

'Not really,' I say, going back to my skipping. 'She probably just left the oven on. Or her car running. Or her front door open. It happens a lot.'

'So what *are* you going to do for *Rainbow Class*

126

Has Talent?' Polly asks me as we skip around the garden.

'Dunno,' I shrug. 'Your song sounded amazing today.'

'Thanks,' Polly smiles. 'But Madame Flounce was right. You need to find something you love and share it with the world.'

I think about all the things I love doing. Maths. Skipping. Eating chocolate. UniMingoes. I don't think they'd make very good talents for the show. There must be something ...

'Hey – that reminds me,' I say, because a more important thought has come into my head. 'Did you see the trailer for *UniMingoes 3*?'

'Yeeeeessss!' squeals Polly. 'It looks SO cool. Did you hear the new song?'

'Yes,' I squeal back, before we sing together, '*UniMingoes, friends together, everybody sing for ever. And for ever. And for ever. And for ever. And for ever ...*'

'Eeeeek!' Polly squeals even louder. 'We have to go see it this weekend. Let's ask my mum.'

'No, let's ask my dad!' I shout back. 'He always lets us have the popcorn with the sweeties on top and fizzy drinks …'

'… and pic 'n' mix and slushies!' Polly cries, throwing her skipping rope over her head. 'This is going to be so—'

'WILL YOU BE QUIET OVER THERE!' a grumpy voice roars over the fence. 'I'M TRYING TO RELAX! I JUST WANT TO COMPOST IN PEACE!'

We look over the fence to where a red-faced Grumpy Barry is putting a big pile of mouldy vegetables in a big barrel. He has some very strange ideas about what is relaxing.

'S-sorry,' stammers Polly, looking really scared.

'Sorry,' I say. (*I'm also really scared, by the way, but the word just comes out right the first time.*)

'I should think so too!' Barry grumbles. 'Some of us just want to enjoy our gardens in peace. Keep it down over there!'

Polly and I look at each other and our skipping ropes. Skipping doesn't seem as much fun now. Nothing's as much fun with Grumpy Barry next door. I want Elsie back. And her cake.

We walk back into the house and Polly runs up to our room. I can hear that Aunty Amara is on the phone.

'… yes, I realise it's short notice, but this is incredibly important,' she says. She sounds like Mum when she's Shouting At The Builders. 'She's moving next week! This can't wait! We need to get this finalised! Today!'

My heart does a belly flop. Aunty Rosa's moving out next week. What happens to Aunty Amara then? Will I still see her? She's my aunty-by-marriage, not my aunty-by-ology (*my mum explained this to me, by the way*), so do I still get to keep her as my aunty? When Mum and Dad got divorced, they told me they would always be my mum and dad. But do you still get to be an aunty when you're not married to one?

Uh-oh. I can feel The Crying coming up my throat again. I look out of the window. The sky is getting darker. I will not cry ...

'Scarlett?' comes a soft voice over my shoulder, followed by a warm hug. 'Are you okay?'

I swallow down the tears. I need some answers.

'What's going on?' I ask Aunty Amara. 'Why are you Shouting At The ... Someone?'

Aunty Amara laughs.

'I must remember that phone calls are as private as a train station round here,' she says.

That's a good simile. But I don't care.

Aunty Amara sits me down at the kitchen table.

'Darling Scarlett,' she says, holding my hand.

'There are lots of things going on at the moment. I wish I could tell you about them, but I promised Aunty Rosa I wouldn't until everything was sorted out. But it's all going to be okay, I promise. These are positive changes we are making.'

My heart belly-flops again. That's just what my parents said when they got divorced. My head thinks about William U. I know he's my worstest enemy in the whole world. But I hope he's okay. Divorce is rubbish (*although Luke in my class got a new puppy, when his mum went to live with the man who cleared their gutters*).

'OWWWWWW!' comes a shout from over the fence.

'That doesn't sound like Elsie,' Aunty Amara says.

'It's not,' says Polly, coming back downstairs. 'That's Grumpy Barry. He just dropped a bag of mouldy potatoes on his foot.'

'He's our new neighbour,' I tell her, rolling my eyes to let her know we don't like him.

'And why is Barry so grumpy?' Aunty Amara asks with a smile, getting up to look for the takeaway leaflets she brought with her and has already lost.

'Because of us playing,' Polly grumbles, slumping on to a chair.

'Oh no – it won't really be that,' says Aunty Amara, looking in the washing machine, which is where she found her glasses last week. 'Emotions don't always come out in the right places.'

'What do you mean?' I ask.

'Well … say you're sad about something,' says Aunty Amara, opening the ironing board. 'Some people might cry about it. But others might feel guilty, or embarrassed, or angry. Barry's only just met you – you can't be the reason he's upset. I'm guessing there's something else happening that's making him grumpy. You just happen to be there.'

I think about this. It makes a lot of sense.

It doesn't get my Frisbee back, though.

My dad walks in the wide-open front door, just as Aunty Amara finds the takeaway leaflets in the dishwasher.

'Hey, everyone,' he says. 'Finished early today, so thought I'd come home and see my girls.'

He hugs Aunty Amara, then Polly and finally me (*but I'm the only one who gets a tickly beard kiss, by the way*).

'I was just going to order a takeaway,' says Aunty Amara, holding the leaflets. 'Only ... I seem to have lost my phone ...'

'Don't worry about it,' Dad says, switching off the oven. 'I'm here now – you get home to Rosa.'

'Rosa's working late tonight,' says Aunty Amara. 'So it'll just be me.'

I start to feel sad again. That sounds like a lie.

'Well, you're very welcome to join us,' Dad says.

'You're sweet – but I have loads to do,' says Aunty Amara. 'There's still … lots to sort out.'

'Oh – of course,' says Dad. 'Er … good luck with … all that.'

(*My dad doesn't always know what to say to people when they're having a hard time, by the way. So he just sort of says some words and hopes that it works.*)

'Thanks,' says Aunty Amara, giving him another hug. 'We're getting there. Let me know if you find my phone.'

'How?' I ask, but it's too late as Aunty Amara has driven off – her car was already running. Dad starts getting us some tea.

'Don't you girls have some homework to do?' he asks suspiciously. 'And don't try telling me that Wednesday's homework is watching TV. Just because I fell for that last term, doesn't mean I'm going to fall for it again …'

I did all my homework in wet play – I nearly

cried at school at lunchtime and it rained again. But Polly gets up from the table with a moan.

'See ya,' she says, trudging up the stairs with her school bag. I pick mine up and see the Memory Book inside. Aunty Amara and Jakub have both given me their memories and I stuck them in with a glue stick and put stickers around them – it looks really good. I wonder if Dad has a special memory of Granny I can stick in my Memory Book.

'Dad?' I ask. 'Do you have a special memory of Granny I can stick in my Memory Book?' (*This seems like the best way of finding out.*)

'Oh, I'm sure I do,' he says, putting a pan on to boil. 'Cheesy pasta okay for tea?'

'Yummy,' I say. (*Dad makes the best cheesy pasta, by the way. It's his own special recipe where he puts cheese on pasta.*)

'So do you have one? A memory?'

Dad stops and leans against the kitchen counter.

136

He starts to laugh.

'Oh, yes I do,' he says. 'The first time I asked your mum out, Emi and I were only seventeen – we were still at school. Nancy demanded I came to the house to speak to her first. She laid down a list of rules – I had to have your mum home by ten p.m., I was to take her somewhere really nice and split the bill.'

'What did you do?'

'I was absolutely terrified!' he grins. 'I'd planned to take your mum for a burger, but with Nancy in my ear, I went and got us a table at the fanciest restaurant in town, where we could only afford a bowl of soup to share. We were home half an hour later! I gave Granny the receipt to prove where we'd been. And on our wedding day your granny gave it back. I still have it in the card upstairs – it made me laugh. It was typical Nancy.'

He shakes his head with a big smile. I like that

the Memory Book is making the adults think about all their happy memories. This was a good idea. Well done, Granny.

Uh-oh …

Thinking about Granny, I get another **BIG FEELING**.

But it's not The Crying this time.

It's my Angry Bubbles.

None of this is fair. I don't want to remember Granny. I want her here with me. Why has she been taken away? And why are Maisie and Mr Nibbles being taken away too? I want to tell my Granny about my **BIG FEELINGS** and ask what I should do for the talent show and I really need my School BFF and her red glasses and I really don't want to get angry as Dad won't know what to say, so I squash down the Angry Bubbles and squash them down and squash them down some more and—

KEEEEERRRRRRRRRRR-SPLAAAAAAAT!!!

There is a big, wet bang and a mouldy old carrot splats all over our kitchen window.

'NOOOOOOO!!!!' comes an angry shout from next door. 'MY COMPOST!!!'

'What was that?!' my dad squeals, like he's just had an allergic reaction to Mr Nibbles.

He comes over to the window with Polly, where we can all see Grumpy Barry covered in exploded old vegetables.

Polly and I try not to giggle. This time I'm definitely the reason that Barry's grumpy. Maybe my **BIG FEELINGS** aren't always so bad.

'Ah,' says Dad, going back to the kitchen. 'Well, that solves *that* mystery.'

I turn round. My dad is holding up the pasta jar with a big smile.

Because inside it is Aunty Amara's phone.

CHAPTER -1 + 10

'Come along, child! I don't have all day!'

I'm standing in the doorway of the big glass room (*called a Drawing Room, by the way, even though I can't see any easels or pineapples or anything – silly Unwords*) at Tottington Hall because today it's my tea with Lady Tottington-Snoot.

I'm not really sure what to do.

When you go for tea with a friend, you usually do something fun first, like hide and seek or face-paints, then you have something nice to eat, like fish fingers or pasta (*or both together if you go to Marcia's house*) and then you watch TV and then your mum walks over to pick you up and says 'we're going in five minutes', then has some

Mummy Juice with your friend's parent and you don't actually leave until it's dark and her dinner is TOTALLY RUINED.

But I don't think this is that kind of tea.

Lady Tottington-Snoot is sitting on her big chair by the glass doors, with all her cats dotted around the room. Maggie, the ginger cat, is pushing one of the other cats out of the basket. Teresa, the beige cat, is fighting with the cats behind her. I wave at Boris, whose fluffy blond fur gives him away as he tries to take the other cats' food while they're not looking.

'I said – come!' Lady Tottington-Snoot commands. This isn't like tea at a friend's house (*although Marcia is quite bossy, by the way, and she has a cat too*) and I can feel the Worry Wobbles in my tummy, which is not good because Lady Tottington-Snoot has lots of stuff that breaks.

'Well, there you are,' says Lady Tottington-

Snoot, not sounding very happy about it. 'Sit down, young lady. I'm very busy.'

She rings a little silver bell next to her and her butler Bertram comes in with a pretty tray, all stacked up like a wedding cake, full of sandwiches and cakes and scones (*which are supposed to be cakes, by the way, but are actually big hard lumps of something a bit like bread that not even cream and jam can save*). It looks delicious and I'm so busy choosing my cake that I feel my Worry Wobbles go away.

'Well, go on then,' says Lady Tottington-Snoot. 'Have your tea. I can't sit around here all afternoon.'

I want to ask what else she is going to do all afternoon because I don't think Lady Tottington-Snoot has a job other than eating tea. But I'm not sure if I should because 1) it might be one of those questions that adults think are rude when you're really just asking a question, and 2) I want a cake much more.

I look at the big tray of cakes. It's a lot for two people.

'Have you got other friends coming round?' I ask her. 'Is this like a double playdate? Because I had one of those with Elizabeth and Tanika,  but Elizabeth's mum had to come and pick her up when Elizabeth and Tanika had a big fight over whose turn it was in Hungry Hippos and Elizabeth said she didn't want to be there any more. But it was a bit awkward because then Tanika's mum and Elizabeth's mum had their "five minutes" on the Mummy Juice and Elizabeth had to sit in the hall in a bad mood on her own. I won that game of Hungry Hippos, by the way.'

Lady Tottington-Snoot looks at me like I just did a botty pop.

'It will just be you and me,' she says.

'But I bet your friends and family love coming to your Big Posh House,' I say. 'We used to go to my aunties' Big Posh House. But since we moved here, everyone comes to us because we're living in your Big Posh House, although my mum says we mustn't brag, even though she really likes telling Aunty Rosa about it all the time and—'

'I do not have any family,' Lady Tottington-Snoot interrupts, which is a bit rude, but adults are allowed. 'And a lady of my status doesn't require friends.'

'Really?' I say. 'But everyone … requires friends. Otherwise who do you do fun stuff with?'

She gives me the botty-pop look again.

'I don't do "fun stuff",' she says, with quite a lot of spit coming out. 'Now, hurry up. I have other things to do besides this.'

Wow. No friends or family. I wouldn't like that – even in a Big Posh House like this. What's the point in even having such a Big Posh House if it's just you in it? Who do you play Hungry Hippos with?

I look around the room. Her butler is pouring the tea. Her maid is dusting the bookshelves. Outside, Jakub is mowing the lawn. Granny always said it was polite to ask questions. So I think now would be a good time to ask my Not Rude question.

'What do you actually do?' I ask her, putting a big cream cake on my plate. I can always have the sandwiches for afters.

'I beg your pardon?' says Lady Tottington-Snoot, peering at me through the little glasses that sit on the end of her nose.

'You keep saying you're really busy,' I say, making sure I'm super polite and wiping the cream off my mouth with my sleeve before speaking. 'But you have lots of people doing stuff for you. So I just wondered what it is you actually do?'

'Impertinent girl,' Lady Tottington-Snoot mutters, taking a tiny cucumber sandwich off the tray and not answering my question.

'Was that question too hard?' I ask her, taking a little doughnut off the tray. 'Because Mum always says I ask impossible questions, like "Who invented builders?" and "How much does the ocean weigh?" But she also says that if you don't ask questions, you won't learn anything. So I think it's a bit like when she tells me I can't eat too much chocolate, but she and Jakub eat a whole box of biscuits when I've gone to bed, but think I don't know about it.'

Lady Tottington-Snoot peers at me again.

'You talk a great deal for one so young,' she says. 'And it's not an impossible question, it's just one I don't care to answer.'

147

'Oh, okay,' I say, taking an iced finger off the tray. 'I understand. Granny says it's rude to ask someone something they might not want to answer. Like when I ask people why they were in the toilet for so long. It's embarrassing, apparently. So if you're embarrassed, that's okay. And you can spend as long as you want in the toilet too.'

'I am not embarrassed!' Lady Tottington-Snoot snaps. 'And I'll thank you to keep your thoughts on … lavatories … to yourself. Your grandmother is a wise lady. You should listen to her.'

I suddenly feel The Crying come up in my throat – this thing just comes out of nowhere. I put back the fruit tart I was holding. I don't want to make it soggy with the tears. And I'm feeling a bit sick.

'I can't,' I say quietly.

'You can't what, child?' asks Lady Tottington-Snoot. 'Speak up!'

 148

'I can't listen to my granny,' I say, my voice starting to wobble as the tears come up. 'Because she died.'

It's too late to keep The Crying out of my throat. Now I have to shut my eyes to stop the tears. Lady Tottington-Snoot probably thinks that's imp-internet like when I asked what she does, but I don't care. I miss my granny. I wish I was having tea and cakes with her. She was never too busy for me. Oh no – I'm swallowing super hard and the black cloud is coming over and now it's going to rain on Jakub outside and …

But then I feel a hand over mine. It makes me jump a little, so I open my eyes and it stops The Crying.

Lady Tottington-Snoot is putting her hand over mine. And she's smiling at me.

'I'm so sorry for your loss,' she says in a gentle voice. 'You must miss your grandmother very much.'

I nod and pick up the fruit tart again. Granny said it was a sin to waste food, so …

'It's so very hard losing someone you love,' she sighs, picking up her tea. 'When my Cyril died three years ago, I was quite lost for a while.'

'He was one of your cats?' I try to remember.

'He was my husband,' she smiles. 'But he wasn't unlike my cats. Sleepy. Naughty. Constantly needed feeding. Loving. Fun. Left hair everywhere …'

I laugh.

'He sounds very nice,' I say.

'He was,' says Lady Tottington-Snoot, taking a quick breath before she sips her tea. I think she might be pushing The Crying down too. I try to think of another question.

'Did he get stuck up trees too?'

Lady Tottington-Snoot laughs and it looks like it's made her crying go away. Laughing seems to win over crying. I must remember that.

'You asked me what I do,' she says, clearing her throat and putting her cup back down. 'Well, my job is managing Tottington Hall. It's a big estate. It needs a lot of work.'

'I know,' I say, taking an extra fruit tart to make sure I've had two of my five a day. 'Jakub works all the time.'

'Who is Jakub?' Lady Tottington-Snoot asks.

'Oh yeah – you call him James,' I say. 'Can I say something about that?'

'I suspect you will anyway.'

'I don't want to be rude or anything – but I think it's a bit rubbish that you don't call him by his real name. It's Jakub. Ya-kub. I know you're very busy, but I think you could learn that. You've got time to do it while someone else is doing all your other work.'

'Duly noted,' she says. I think she might be smiling. That's weird. 'But you were saying about his workload.'

'Oh, yeah,' I say through a mouthful of sandwich. 'So Jakub gets up at six a.m., works until at least six p.m. and lots of the weekends too. He says that his work is never done.'

'Is he unhappy with his new job?' Lady Tottington-Snoot asks.

'No,' I say, blowing on my tea to make it cold.

'Good,' she replies.

'But I am,' I point out.

Because I am. A lot.

'I beg your pardon?' she says again, peering down the glasses again.

'Jakub loves his job,' I say, slurping my tea super politely. 'But I love Jakub. And now he's working all the time, I don't get to play with him as much. And he never has time to build our treehouse. And he really wants the treehouse.'

'I see,' says Lady Tottington-Snoot, sipping her

tea again. 'Your mother is expecting, is she not?'

'Yes,' I nod. 'She's expecting the builders to come at four o'clock, but they never turn up when they say they will, which is why she shouts at them so much.'

'You misunderstand,' says Lady Tottington-Snoot. 'I was referring to her ... delicate condition.'

I'm confused. But I think about my granny and not asking people why they've spent so long in the toilet.

'Oh – you mean her massive tummy,' I whisper. 'She's pregnant. With twins. She doesn't need a poo, if that's what you were worried about.'

Lady Tottington-Snoot chokes slightly on her tea before mopping her mouth with a little napkin.

'Thank you, dear, for the clarification,' she says. 'Yes, I was referring to her pregnancy. I wasn't aware that there are two bundles of joy on the way.'

'Uh-huh,' I say, looking at the meringues, although I don't want to be greedy. 'And with Jakub working all the time, she's a bit worried about how she's going to manage them.'

'Babies are a great deal of work,' Lady Tottington-Snoot says.

I nod.

But I was actually talking about the builders.

'I must say,' says Lady Tottington-Snoot, 'I wasn't aware the grounds were so challenging. My previous groundskeeper never mentioned it.'

 154

'Where is he now?' I ask.

'Oh – he left,' she says. 'Something about stress, nervous exhaustion, chronic back pain and divorce. But it sounds like Jakub needs some help.'

I nod a lot.

'Yes – I think that would really help him,' I say. 'And it would keep your garden even nicer if there were two people working on it.'

'Then it is settled,' she says. 'Tell your Jakub that he may start looking for an assistant. And that he must build your treehouse. That is an order.'

She returns to her tea. Lady Tottington-Snoot is much nicer than I thought. So why is she so angry all the time? I think back to what Aunty Amara said about feelings coming out in the wrong places. Maybe Lady Tottington-Snoot isn't angry at all. But if she's got no friends and family – maybe she's a bit lonely.

Thinking of Aunty Amara gives me another idea.

'Lady Tottington-Snoot?' I ask her. 'This is a really nice, light room.'

'It is,' she agrees.

'Perfect for doing some art,' I point out. 'Oh – is that why it's called the Drawing Room?'

Lady Tottington-Snoot laughs.

'Something like that,' she says.

'Well, the thing is, my Aunty Amara – she's super nice, by the way – is looking for somewhere for her Over-Sixties art therapy group. It's full of really nice Over-Sixties like Sadie, who draw pineapples. They meet every week in the library. But the library is getting shut down.'

'I know – it's a tragedy,' says Lady Tottington-Snoot. 'I gave the council a big piece of my mind about that.'

'Oh – okay,' I say. 'Well, with the bit of your

mind that's left – would it be okay if my aunty's art group came here for their art?'

'Well … I … um … I don't …' Lady Tottington-Snoot blusters.

'Pleeeeeeaaaaase,' I say (*because it's always worth trying*). 'Sadie and her Over-Sixties friends love their art and some of them are really lonely and if they don't have their art group, they won't see anyone and I did rescue your cat and—'

'All right, all right,' says Lady Tottington-Snoot, raising a hand. 'They can come here on a trial basis. Put your aunt in touch with me and we'll make suitable arrangements.'

'Wow – thanks!' I say (*because I didn't really think she'd agree*). 'You are so much nicer than everyone says you are.'

Lady Tottington-Snoot laughs again. She does a cheers on my teacup with hers.

'Well, here's to you, Miss Scarlett,' she says.

'Art group or no art group, I have a feeling that
life is going to be rather more colourful with
you around.'

Chapter √100

It's very strange being back at Granny's house.

I always really loved coming to Granny's house, but now I think that might have been because Granny was in it. Without her, it's just a house. A house that doesn't have my granny in it any more.

I'm helping Mum and Aunty Rosa clear all of Granny's things out of it, so that they can sell it. I'm not very happy about someone else living in my granny's house, but Maisie told me to think how happy it will make someone else who doesn't have a nice home. So I thought about that.

And it turns out that I'm REALLY not happy about someone else living in my granny's house.

'You have got to be kidding me,' says Aunty Rosa, pulling a shiny little dress out of a wardrobe.

'There is no way our cardigan-loving, trouser-wearing mother ever wore this.'

She holds the dress up and it just about covers the top half of her body. I can't imagine Granny in it either. She must have needed a really big cardigan when it got 'a bit nippy' (*cold*).

'I'm starting to think there are a lot of things we didn't know about our mother,' says Mum, who is supposed to be sorting a big box of photos, but is actually just looking through a big box of photos. 'Did you know she went to Mount Everest?'

'Yeah – she wanted to prove to her male colleagues at the university that mountain-climbing wasn't just for men,' says Aunty Rosa, pulling more clothes out of the wardrobe. 'She made it halfway up! She was furious she never made it to the top.'

'Was it too much for her?' Mum asks.

'Was it heck!' scoffs Aunty Rosa. 'One of the

male history professors got a blister on his little toe and said he couldn't carry on! She was still angry when she told me the story forty years later.'

I look at the picture of my very young granny standing on a mountain. I like that she was formidable then too.

'Oh,' says Mum, putting her hand to her chest. 'I can't believe she kept this …'

She pulls out a piece of paper and turns it round so we can see it. It's a letter, written in crayon, with a picture of a flower at the bottom. It says:

Deer Mummie,

Eye am sorry I woz norty.

I luv yoo,
Emi

'Awww,' says Aunty Rosa. 'What terrible crime had you committed? Other than your spelling.'

Mum tries to swat Aunty Rosa with a pack of photos (*photos used to come in little folders, by the way. I don't know how people put them back into their phones*). But Mum's too big and Aunty Rosa is too quick.

'I remember this like it was yesterday,' says Mum. 'Granny had baked brownies – huge chocolate fudge brownies – for the school bake sale and left them to cool on the windowsill. I asked her if I could have one and she said no.'

'So you ate one anyway?' I ask.

Mum giggles.

'So I ate all of them anyway,' she says, a naughty twinkle in her eye. 'The whole plate! Granny came back downstairs and asked me what happened and I said I didn't know. So she said, "Anyone who tells a lie has not a pure heart …"'

 162

"'… and cannot make a good soup,'" I finish. Granny used to say that to me when I told a fib. Apparently, a very famous musician called Beethoven said that and it's never made sense to me. But knowing what I know about these brownies and Mum's cooking, now I think I understand.

'I had chocolate all over my face and all over my dress, but I still insisted I wasn't the culprit,' Mum says, her eyes starting to get wet. 'I was sent to my room without any supper – which was a good thing as I was feeling sick from all the brownies – and I wrote this note to say sorry. I pushed it under the door and she came upstairs and gave me a big cuddle for telling the truth at last. I'm amazed she kept it.'

'I'm not that surprised,' says Aunty Rosa. 'It's probably the only living proof of you ever admitting you were wrong.'

'That's not true!' my mum exclaims (*it really is, by the way*).

She tries to hit Aunty Rosa with the photos again. And misses her. Again.

'Urgh – I can't throw all this away,' says Mum. 'But it seems such a shame for it to gather dust in the loft.'

'Why don't you make your own memory book with all those photos, then you can look at it when you're sad and remember how formidable Granny was?' I suggest. 'But – can I have that letter? For my Memory Book?'

Mum's eyes are really full of crying now (*although this isn't unusual, by the way. Since she's been pregnant, she cries at everything. She's worse than Fleur*).

'I think that's a lovely idea, baby,' she says, handing it over. 'I'll make my own memory book. And you put this in yours. Come here.'

We have a big cuddle, which is a bit snotty but I don't mind. I don't know why Mum is so surprised her mummy kept all this stuff. She keeps everything

I make and write and give her – all the pasta pictures and models out of toilet rolls and bracelets made from bits of string – they're all in a Very Special Box in the attic that I'm not allowed to see until I'm fifty.

We come out of our cuddle, because Aunty Rosa is making a strange sound. I turn round and she's sitting on the floor, holding one of Granny's cardigans to her face.

'It still smells of her,' she says, the tears running down her face. 'I can't ... I can't believe she's not here ...'

'Oh, sis,' says Mum, struggling up off the floor to go and give her little sister a cuddle. I don't know what to do. I've never seen Aunty Rosa cry before. I didn't think she knew how. Aunty Rosa is strong and powerful and nothing scares her. Seeing her crying in my mum's arms is really weird. I don't like it. I can feel my own crying wanting to join in. My crying seems to think if it's okay for a big, strong grown-up like Aunty Rosa to cry, then it's okay for me to do it too. But my crying is wrong. I am NOT going to cry. What if I really can't stop?

I see the dark clouds start to gather outside. The talent show is only a few days away. I have to learn to control this or I'm going to ruin it for everyone.

'Aunty Rosa,' I say gently, trying to think of something nicer (*this seems to be working well, by the way*). 'Do you have something I could put in the Memory Book? A letter? Even if it's spelled as badly as Mum's, I don't mind.'

Aunty Rosa laughs and her whole face lights up. The cloud passes over – laughing wins again. She blows her nose, stands up and goes to Granny's dressing table (*which is nothing to do with dressing up, by the way, as I found out when I went looking for something for my Dress As A Vegetable Day at school and Granny told me off for being a Nosy Parker*).

'Well ... I was never really one for writing letters or drawing pictures,' she says. 'But there is one thing that will always make me think of Granny.'

Aunty Rosa picks up a bottle of perfume from the table and sprays a little bit on her wrist. She holds it up to her nose and closes her eyes.

'Mum,' she whispers, some smiling tears coming to her eyes. My mum smells it too and they stand with their arms around each other. It's nice to see them getting along – Granny would be very happy that they're not squabbling (*which was her Polite Olden Days way of saying 'fighting', by the way*). Maybe now they've both got Big Posh Houses, they'll get on a bit better.

'Here, squidge,' she says, coming towards me. 'Hold your Memory Book open.'

I take the book out of my bag and open a new page. Aunty Rosa holds the perfume a little way away, then sprays three squirts all over the book, before tucking in the picture of young Granny on Mount Everest.

'There,' she says, as the smell of my granny's perfume fills my book and my nose. 'That's my memory. That's what I think of when I think of my mum.'

I smell the book again. Now it really smells like my granny. I love that.

Aunty Rosa smiles at Mum, then comes and gives me a big hug. She looks much happier now she's got all the crying out. Maybe that's what crying does. Maybe it helps you to wash all the sad out. Maybe it gets all the tears out of your head and on to a tissue. Maybe it's a way to express all the feelings that silly Unwords can't say.

That's interesting.

I'm still not doing it, though.

ChAPTER 22 ÷ 2

'You *must* have figured out what your talent is by now?' Polly asks me as we play catch in Dad's garden with Maisie, who has come over for a playdate. '*Rainbow Class Has Talent* is in two days!'

I shake my head. I can feel the Worry Wobbles in my tummy. The talent show is the day after tomorrow. Karam has finished his poem now, so I'm the only one who doesn't know what I'm going to do. Or if I'm going to TOTALLY RUIN everything by making a thunderstorm. Or if Jakub can even come with all the work he has to do at Tottington Hall – he hasn't managed to find an assistant yet, so he's still working super hard all the time (*and we still don't have our treehouse, by the way*).

'You'll think of something,' says Maisie. 'You always do. Perhaps we can help you?'

I smile at my School BFF. Maisie's foster family had to change their plans to fly to Australia by a week, so she can do the talent show, which is super good news. But a few days later she has to move to a new family and she still doesn't know who or where that family is. She says she doesn't want to talk about it. I think her red glasses are having to work super hard to keep their perspective right now.

'Yes, let's do that,' says Polly. 'So we need something that you love, something you care about and something that you want to share with the whole world.'

'What about your badge collection?' Maisie suggests, throwing the ball to me.

'Nope,' I say, catching it and throwing it on to Polly. 'I only ever collected three badges, then

swapped them with Emma R for her cheese and onion crisps.'

'What about that certificate you got for adopting a panda?' Polly says, catching the ball.

'Oh,' I say, pulling an embarrassed face. 'I … a little bit … tore that all up when I realised that I didn't actually get to keep the panda in my house … I'm telling you, I haven't got something I love, something I care about and something I want to share with the world.'

I stop.

A Big Idea has just come into my head.

Could I do *that* as my talent?

Maybe I could … ?

'Girls!' Rita shouts from the house. 'Come inside and get your stuff together. Jakub will be here in a minute!'

I burp a little bit. Rita let us make pizzas for tea, which was super awesome as then we could put all the things we want on top of ours. I wanted cheese, tomato, ham and jelly beans, but Rita said maybe I should keep the jelly beans on the side and now I think she was probably right.

'Scarlett! Catch!' says Polly, throwing the ball really, really high. I step backwards to catch it – I'm *very* good at catching – but just as I'm about to jump for the ball, my feet get tangled in the skipping ropes we said we'd tidy up three days ago and I fall on my bum. I watch as the ball flies over the fence … and into Barry's garden.

'Great,' I say grumpily. 'Now we won't ever see that ball again, just like the pink Frisbee.'

But just as I'm getting ready to fold my arms to show how cross I am, the ball comes flying back over the fence. Polly, Maisie and I stare at each other in confusion. Has Grumpy Barry stopped being grumpy? And we're even more confused when a head pops up over the fence and it isn't on

Grumpy Barry. It's on a very smiley lady.

'Hi, girls,' she says with a cheery wave. 'There's your ball. Nice to meet you at last.'

I'm very confused.

'I'm very confused,' Polly says, because she must be very confused too. 'Where's Barry?'

'Oh – Barry's not here,' smiles the lady. 'I'm Sheila.'

Polly and I smile at each other – this is great news!

'Has Barry moved into a home, like Elsie did?' I ask.

Sheila bursts out laughing.

'Not yet,' she says. 'But if he doesn't stop leaving his socks on the floor, I might take him to one myself. Do you know, we've been married for thirty-two years?!'

I try not to look at Polly, as I know she's thinking the same thing I am.

'Why?' I say, before I realise I've said it out loud.

Sheila laughs again. 'I ask myself that question some days,' she says. 'Believe me! Oh – here you go. I found this in our shed. I don't think it's Barry's.'

She throws over the pink Frisbee.

'Wow, thanks!' Polly says to Nice Sheila.

'You're welcome,' smiles Sheila. 'You'll have to excuse Barry. He's a lovely man. But he's a bit of a grump at the moment.'

'We hadn't noticed,' I say, because that's the sort of lie you're supposed to tell in moments like this.

'Well, that's very kind of you to say,' smiles Sheila. 'But he's been like a bear with a sore head (*nice simile*) ever since he stopped working. He loved his job at the bank.'

'So why did he stop doing it?' Polly asks. 'Was it because he was a bit grumpy?'

'I don't think so,' smiles Sheila. 'No, someone

newer and younger came along and they didn't want Barry doing that job any more.'

'Oh,' I say. 'That's rubbish.'

'Yes,' Sheila agrees. 'Really rubbish. Rubbish for Barry because he's bored and grumpy. And rubbish for me because I've got a bored and grumpy husband!'

'And rubbish for us because he takes our stuff and gets grumpy at us,' I point out.

'Well, yes,' smiles Sheila. 'But don't you worry – if it happens again, just come and see me. It's lovely to hear the sound of children playing next door. Our grandchildren live a long way away, so we don't get to see and hear them that much. And all our friends are back where we used to live.'

A Good Idea comes into my head.

'Are you an Over-Sixty?' I ask her, remembering a bit too late that Granny said it wasn't polite to ask people their ages, which is weird, because they always ask you at Mr Blister's Soft Play if you're really old enough to go on the zip wire, even when you're not and you have to fib.

Sheila laughs.

'Just,' she says.

'And do you like drawing pineapples?' I ask her.

Sheila laughs some more.

'I haven't done any drawing for years. I used to really enjoy it, though.'

'Then I know somewhere you can draw pineapples AND make friends,' I tell her. 'I'll get my Aunty Amara to tell you all about it next time she's here.'

'Well, that sounds wonderful, thank you,' says Sheila. 'And I must say, it's lovely knowing you girls are having fun. You carry on. Whatever Barry has to say about it.'

Polly and I smile. We like Nice Sheila.

'Well,' sighs Nice Sheila, looking behind her.

177

'At least my garden is getting done. That's the only thing Barry seems to enjoy about being retired – more time to spend in the garden. I just wish we had a bigger one. This one will be done soon and then he'll be under my feet again.'

Now a Very Brilliant Idea comes into my head.

'So Grumpy … er … Barry really likes gardening?' I ask her.

'Loves it,' says Sheila. 'He'd do it all day if he could.'

'And he's missing his job?'

'Very much,' sighs Sheila. 'My husband needs something useful to do. All husbands need something useful to do …'

'Hey, squidge!' I hear Jakub yelling up the garden. 'Time to go.'

I smile at Nice Sheila and then at Jakub.

I think I might get my treehouse after all.

ChAPTER 11 + 13 - 12

School shows are always really exciting because:

1) You don't have to do normal school
2) You get to wear Own Clothes
3) All the parents come and watch
4) We always go for ice cream afterwards

But today I'm worried about what I'm doing. My talent isn't like Polly's singing, or Azuri's gymnastics, or Roshin's shadow puppets. I've just got something I love, something I care about and something I want to share with the world. But what if I'm rubbish? What if everyone laughs at me? What if The Crying starts to come up my throat and I make a storm cloud and the whole marquee collapses?

I look up to the roof – we're in the marquee now, waiting behind a curtain. It's a nice sunny evening, but even then, the marquee wobbles every time someone walks through the door. There's no way it will stay up if my **BIG FEELINGS** make a thunderstorm. I feel the Worry Wobbles in my tummy and the marquee starts to rock. I do some alphabet game to calm myself down and they stop. I'm going to have to be very careful tonight.

Everyone is looking out of the curtain to see their parents, who are waving at us, even though Madame Flounce keeps pulling the curtain back over us and tells us to stay out of sight (*which is a bit weird, by the way, because it's not like our parents don't know we're here, and would probably be a bit worried if we weren't*).

Felix is waving at his dads. Roshin is waving

at her mum, her uncle, both her brothers and at least three grandparents (*Roshin has a really big family, by the way*). Maisie's foster mum and dad blow her a kiss and Maisie waves back. Maisie's foster mum is already crying – they are very sad at having to leave Maisie behind for their new life in Australia. They wanted to take Maisie with them, but that's not allowed. I'm glad they get to see her in the talent show, though. Maisie is going to do a drawing (*she is SUPER good at Art, by the way*) and I'm happy they'll all have a nice memory together.

I see Mum and Jakub and Dad and Rita come in together, laughing. They often go to the pub for dinner before my school shows, which is a bit like us going for ice cream afterwards. They all wave and Polly and I are about to wave back, when my aunties rush in and say something to them. They are all getting very excited. Everyone is gasping and jigging up and down like they need a wee.

'What's going on?' Polly asks.

'I don't know,' I say, trying to lean my head nearer so I can hear, when I'm distracted by someone barging past me.

It's William U. Of course.

'Don't be such a meanie,' I say.

'Move out the way, stinky,' he snarls at me as he opens the curtain. William U's mum is looking towards the door, but there's an empty seat next to her. She sees William U and she waves harder than any of the other parents wave, but William U doesn't wave back. He's just looking at the empty chair. He slams the curtain back and barges past us again.

'Move!' he shouts, his voice a little bit croaky.

I look at the empty chair.

Ah.

I see.

For once, I think I understand What's Upsetting William.

He has a big space where someone should be too.

'Places, children, places!' gasps Madame Flounce, whose scarves are all over the place tonight. 'Curtain in five minutes! That's five minutes!'

I look at the flap at the back of the marquee. William U hasn't said one nice thing to me for ages. But, as Granny always said, 'an eye for an eye and the world will go blind'. I'm not going to poke William U in the eye. But perhaps I can help him.

I walk out of the marquee and find him sitting at the back on the grass, his head on his knees. His shoulders are shaking, which could mean he's a) very cold, or b) finds something very funny, but I don't think that's what's happening here. I go and sit down next to him.

'Go away,' he says, but not as hard as he would normally say it, so I stay.

'We're about to start,' I tell him. 'And your tightrope act is first.'

'I don't care,' he says, wiping his nose with his sleeve. 'I don't care about Stupid Rainbow Class Has Stupid Talent. It's stupid.'

'But … you really wanted to go first,' I point out. 'You got your mum to write a letter. And have a meeting with Madame Flounce. And donate a big prize to the PSA raffle. And—'

'It doesn't matter now,' sniffs William U. 'I'm not doing it.'

I try to think of a way to ask if it's because his dad isn't here.

'Is it because your dad isn't here?' I ask, because this is no time for silly Unwords.

William U doesn't say anything. He breathes a few times, like he's trying to push The Crying back down his throat. But the tears won't be pushed. He starts having a really big cry. I don't say anything for a minute. Maybe he needs to wash his sad away.

'When my mum and dad got divorced, they told me that families are like Lego,' I tell him. 'All different shapes and sizes. They might get broken up, but they can be put together again in all kinds of new and better ways. Which is weird, by the way, because both my mum and my dad are rubbish at Lego and keep saying that the instructions are wrong on the pirate ship I got four years ago. But I think I understand what they mean.'

William U sniffs into his arms.

'Your family is going to be a different shape,' I tell him. 'It might not be the shape you're used to. But it's still a family. And it could be new and better.'

William U lifts up his head.

'Well, it's not much of a family if my dad isn't here,' he says in little bits as his tears are still in the way.

I wrinkle up my nose (*that means I don't agree, by the way*).

'Yes, it is,' I remind him. 'You and your mum will always be a family. If your dad doesn't join in, he's the one who's missing out. You can't be a family on your own. Divorce makes grown-ups quite angry and really very stupid. Once he stops being angry and stupid, I bet he'll want to be your dad properly again.'

'He doesn't want to be my dad properly tonight,' William U sniffs.

'And that's really rubbish,' I agree. 'He's made a big mistake. But this show isn't about your dad. It's about sharing your talent with everyone. And there are lots of people who want to see that.'

'Like who?' William U grumbles.

'Like Madame Flounce,' I say. 'And Ms Pitt-Bull. And your mum. She's already made the people in front of her move out the way so she can film you. And ... and me. I want to see your act too.'

'Really?' he asks. 'Why? We're not even friends.'

'We used to be,' I shrug. 'You used to come to my house all the time. And if you stop calling me names, we could be friends again. And ... honestly, I kinda thought it was the right thing to say to make you happy.'

William U smiles.

'You have to go on stage,' I say, as we both hear Madame Flounce scream William's name in the

188

marquee. 'Just think of all the money your mum spent on that chocolate hamper for the raffle.'

We both laugh.

'You can't do anything about your parents,' I say to him. 'But you can do something for you. And I think going on stage and sharing your talent would be a really good thing for you to do.'

William U wipes his eyes, stands up and wipes the grass off his bum (*sorry, Granny*).

'Okay,' he says. 'I'll do it.'

'Good,' I say, wiping the grass off my ... rear end too. 'You're supposed to say "break a leg" when someone goes on stage, but given your act, that would be a bad idea ...'

William U smiles and goes towards the flap in the marquee.

'Thanks, Scarlett,' he says quietly. 'Perhaps you're not so stinky after all.'

He goes inside, where I hear Madame Flounce

scream his name and rush him to the stage. That felt good. That was the right thing to do.

And who knows?

It might even give me a better chance at winning the chocolate hamper in the PSA raffle.

Chapter 14 - 7

The talent show is going really well. William U's tightroping went so well, his mum gave it a standing ovation before it had even started. Felix caught all his tomatoes. Vashti made a bouquet of paper flowers and gave them to Ms Pitt-Bull. Polly's song was AMAZING and Maisie drew a picture of her foster family for them to take to Australia, which made everyone cry.

Now it's Karam's turn.

Maisie and Karam have been working on his poem, but Maisie says that Karam didn't really need much help, except when he had to spell the word 'language', which Maisie and I couldn't spell either because it doesn't look anything like it sounds (*silly Unwords*). Karam's whole family have come to support him and cheer super loud as he comes on stage. He smiles and holds up his piece of paper.

'I'm going to read a poem,' he says. 'I'd like to thank my friend Scarlett for trying to help me and my friend Maisie for actually helping me.'

The grown-ups laugh. Maisie and I grin at each other. It feels good to help. I just wish I could help Mr Nibbles, who still doesn't have a forever home. Just like Maisie …

Karam stands up tall to read his poem.

'My poem is called "Everyone Speaks Smile".'

He shakes his paper out and starts to read:

You might not know your German
Or said French in a while
But there's one thing we understand
As everyone speaks Smile

Smiling is a language
That everyone can know
You move your lips into a grin
And no one will feel low

Words take time to master
A language has no end
But if you have a great big smile
You'll always find a friend

So whether you're from Asia
Or grew up near the Nile
Let's use the thing we all can know
Cos everyone speaks Smile

The marquee goes super quiet. Did the adults not like the poem? Because I thought it was SUPER brilliant.

Suddenly an almighty roar goes up from the audience. All the adults are on their feet, clapping and cheering, Karam's family are in tears as the other parents hug them and pat their backs – and most importantly …

Everyone is smiling.

Great job, Karam. Maisie looks super proud and is clapping mega hard.

Karam comes off the stage and goes back to playing dinosaurs with William D. They are Best Forever Friends (*at school and I think at home too*). The parents are still clapping.

I feel the Worry Wobbles start in my tummy. It's not long until my turn and I still don't know that I've chosen the right thing. I can feel them starting to come out of me and the marquee starts to wobble. Oh no, it's starting, I can't—

'Scarlett? Are you all right?'

The voice distracts me from my wobbles. It's Ms Pitt-Bull. And she's looking at me with a smile.

'Yes,' I say, but then remember that an important part of stopping the Worry Wobbles is to talk about my worries. 'No.'

'Anything I can help with?' says Ms Pitt-Bull, tilting her head to the side.

'I'm worried about my talent,' I say, as she takes us over to two chairs. 'I don't think it's as good as everyone else's.'

'I'm sure that's not the case,' says Ms Pitt-Bull. 'I think that one of the wonderful things about today is that we're seeing how everyone is talented in their own special way. So your way will be different, but just as special as everyone else's.'

'Maybe,' I say, which means I'm not sure about that at all, but I don't want to be rude.

'Would you like to show me?' she offers, and

that seems like a really good idea. I pull my piece of paper out and hand it to her. Ms Pitt-Bull reads it and smiles.

'Oh, Scarlett. I think that this is very wonderful,' she says, looking like The Crying might be in her throat too. 'And I just know that everyone else will agree.'

'Okay,' I say. That does make me feel better. Ms Pitt-Bull is a teacher and she's been to Teacher University to understand what's good and what isn't, so if she thinks it's good, then it must be.

'Scarlett, I overheard what you said to William earlier,' she says.

'Oh,' I say. 'Well, I thought "meanie" was better than "bum-head" or "poo-face" or any of the other things I wanted to say when he barged past me.'

'And you were correct,' Ms Pitt-Bull smiles. 'But I wasn't referring to that. I was talking about what you said outside the marquee. When he was upset.'

'Am I in trouble?' I ask. 'I know you shouldn't stick your nose where it doesn't belong – which is weird, because it's not like your nose can come off your face – but I understand a bit about how William U feels because my parents got a divorce and—'

Ms Pitt-Bull holds up her hands. This means 'be quiet' in teacher talk. I'm guessing you learn that at Teacher University too.

'You're not in any trouble,' she promises. 'Quite the reverse, in fact. I thought it was an incredibly kind thing to do.'

'Oh,' I say. 'That's good then.'

'Really, Scarlett,' she says. 'I know that you and William can have a … challenging relationship. So for you to reach out to him like that was very generous. And I know he will have appreciated it too.'

'I know,' I say. 'He said I'm not that stinky.'

Ms Pitt-Bull laughs.

'Well, there you go then. That's progress,' she says as the parents applaud Fleur's tap-dancing and she bursts into tears. 'Well now – I think that's your cue. Good luck.'

'Don't you mean "break a leg"?' I ask her as we walk to the side of the stage.

Ms Pitt-Bull looks up at the rickety marquee.

'No,' she says quietly. 'I really don't.'

'And now,' Madame Flounce announces into the microphone, 'it is time for our final act of the evening. But before we hear from Scarlett, I have a little announcement of my own.'

Here we go. What is St Lidwina's going to be the Centre for now?

'Wonderful as my guest appearance at St Lidwina's has been, my heart will forever belong to the stage,' Madame Flounce sort of sings. 'So when an opportunity arose to star in a touring production of *The Bride of Frankenstein*, I had to follow the call. I will be leaving the school with immediate effect.'

The adults groan. Felix grumpily hands Rory his KitKat.

'However, you will be pleased to know that the post of Head has already been filled and my replacement will be starting on Monday. The new head teacher of St Lidwina's Primary School will be ...'

I turn to Ms Pitt-Bull and whisper, 'Great. At least if we don't like them, they probably won't be here very long,' I say.

'Oh, I think this one's here to stay,' she smiles back with a wink. I didn't know Ms Pitt-Bull could wink. Today is full of surprises. I turn back to Madame Flounce, who is taking a really long time to say one name. It can't really take this much—

'MS PITT-BULL!'

WHAT?!

I turn back to Ms Pitt-Bull, who is smiling very happily. And I'm happy too.

Finally.

A head teacher who wants St Lidwina's to be a Centre for Really Happy Children.

I don't really know why I do it.

But I throw my arms around Ms Pitt-Bull and give her a massive hug.

And I'm not the only who is happy. The adults look like they've already been to the pub. They all clap and cheer and shout her name.

'Shall we?' asks Ms Pitt-Bull, taking my hand.

'Okay,' I say, and we walk on to the stage together. The adults are still clapping and cheering, and after ages, Ms Pitt-Bull has to put up her 'be quiet' hands (*which works on adults too, by the way. That Teacher University is good*).

'Thank you. Thank you,' says Ms Pitt-Bull, who looks like she is starting to blush a bit. 'You are very kind. As I'm sure you can imagine, I am delighted and excited to take up my new post and there is much for us to discuss after all the ... uncertainties of the past year. But tonight belongs to my wonderful Rainbow Class – and I'm sure you will all agree, Rainbow Class *really* Has Talent.'

The adults clap and whoop again. They are in a

really good mood. We're getting loads of ice cream later.

'But we have one act remaining,' says Ms Pitt-Bull, looking down at me. 'I am so proud of everyone in my class; they have all excelled themselves tonight. And I'm very proud of our final act too. I have watched this little rainbow shine in the face of all kinds of challenges over the past year, always with courage and always with kindness. She has something very special to share with you tonight, so it is my great pleasure to introduce the very brilliant … Scarlett Fife!'

All the adults clap and Ms Pitt-Bull lets go of my hand with a squeeze and walks off the stage. I feel all the Worry Wobbles bubble up again. There are lights shining in my eyes and suddenly the marquee feels very big. I look out into the audience and all my parents are there, giving me thumbs-ups and blowing me kisses.

'Um … so, I didn't really know what to do today,' I start saying, pulling my paper out of my pocket. 'I don't have a talent for bird whistles, like Parva, or speaking another language, like Milly, or burping the alphabet, like my stepdad.'

The adults laugh. Although not Jakub so much.

'But Madame Flounce told us to think of something we love, something we care about and something we want to share with everyone,' I carry on. 'The first thing I thought of was chocolate, but it's quite hard to share that in a big marquee.'

Everyone laughs again. I don't know why.

'So I thought of something else I love. Something I really care about. And something I want to share with everyone. And that something … is my granny.'

I look over at my mum. She's crying, but that's pretty normal now. Rita takes one hand and Jakub takes the other. Aunty Amara hugs Aunty Rosa.

203

My dad pats them both on the back.

'So my granny was called Nancy Andrews. She was born in 1945, which was the year the Second World War ended. I used to think that maybe my granny helped to stop the Second World War because she was formidable and very good at telling people how to behave.'

Everyone laughs again.

'I don't know lots about what happened next because it was in the olden days when people didn't have Instagram and Facebook to tell everyone what they were doing all day. But I do know that she went to university when people didn't think girls should go and she became a teacher so that she could make sure that more girls went to university. She was married to my Grandad Reg, who also taught at university and used to leave his teeth out for us to find, although I don't think that's why she married him.'

More laughing. I turn round. Is someone making funny faces behind my back or something?

'Anyway – then she had my mum and my Aunty Rosa. She told me that they were her proudest achievement, which is pretty impressive because she once won the gold medal at the village fete for her Eccles cakes. But for me, her greatest achievement was being The Best Granny in the World, which she was to me …'

Uh-oh. I can feel The Crying coming up again. The sky starts to darken. I am NOT going to cry …

'My granny was good at lots of things. She made really good cakes, told really good stories and even made boring things like museums and nature walks really interesting and fun. She wasn't good at everything – she thought flossing was something you did to your teeth. And she never did learn to use her phone – she could only use it to call people, bless her.'

I look out in the audience and everyone is smiling at me. All except for Mum. Mum is full-on crying now. That makes my tears come harder. But I want to finish what I'm saying about my granny. I can hear spots of rain falling on the marquee. I don't have long.

'My granny died not very long ago,' I say, and everyone goes very quiet. 'She asked me to make this Memory Book, which I'm doing because she told me to and she's still formidable. All my family have given me things to put in. But I've been really stuck what to put in myself because I have so many memories. There was the time she took me to the zoo and ended up starting a petition to free all the animals. And the time she taught me Bad Choice Words in Latin. And all the times she helped me, made me laugh and gave me sweets. So I'm going to put this thing I'm reading now in the Memory Book. Because I want to share my memories of my granny with you. Because I love her. And I care about her. And I wish … I wish … I wish…'

I keep trying to push The Crying down. But this time it is just too strong. I take a deep breath.

'And I wish she was here so I could share her with you now,' I say, before the tears burst out of my throat, nose, eyes and everywhere else they can find.

I AM going to cry.

I'm crying right now.

That's it. I've ruined *Rainbow Class Has Talent*. There is a massive black cloud over the marquee that is going to burst any minute. And everyone will think I'm silly for crying on stage. That's why no one's clapping.

But then one person starts to clap. I look at my family. They are far too busy crying to clap. In fact, everyone in the tent is crying. What's happened?

But whoever is clapping keeps going. It's coming

from the side of the stage, which is where we all have to sit when it's not our turn. I look around to see who it is. I can't believe it …

It's William U.

He's standing up and smiling and clapping. And then Polly and Maisie and Karam stand up and clap. And then all my other friends in Rainbow Class stand up and clap (*except for Fleur, who is too busy crying, and Freddie, who wasn't really listening*). And Madame Flounce is clapping and now all the parents are standing up and everyone is clapping. I feel a rub on my shoulder and a tissue in my hand. Ms Pitt-Bull is standing next to me. And now she is clapping too. She hands me a tissue and I wipe the tears away. I feel much better already.

So yes, I did cry.

But I also stopped.

I look up at the sky – those black clouds looked ready to burst.

But the black clouds have gone. The rain hasn't come. The sun is shining.

And right over the marquee, a beautiful rainbow is beaming.

I start to feel better. And I realise something that's probably quite important, actually.

Crying doesn't make the rain come.

It helps the sun to shine again.

That's the kind of thing my granny would have told me.

Thanks, Granny. You helped me again. I think the fact that I got to have you will always help me.

I miss you.

I love you.

And I really want an ice cream.

Chapter 28 ÷ 2

After the talent show, loads of Rainbow Class and their families go to The Long Arms, which has a big garden with a climbing frame, a slide, three swings and a zip wire (*which is everyone's favourite, by the way*). It also does the best ice cream, which is why the grown-ups bring us here and then they can drink orange juice or wine.

I'm still waiting for Maisie, as her foster family needed to speak to Ms Pitt-Bull after the show. I'm worried what it's about. I hope that it's not because she's moving schools. I look around to distract myself while I wait my turn on the zip wire. My mum and Rita are sitting with William U's mum (*who has drunk a lot more wine than*

orange juice, by the way) and they are giving her lots of cuddles as the music plays in the garden.

'You are a strong, smart, independent woman,' Rita says. 'Yes, you've been a wife and a mother. But you're also … Sorry, I don't think I actually know your name?' (*Rita hasn't drunk much orange juice either.*)

'Sarah,' says William U's mum tearfully. 'My name is SARAH!'

'Yes, it is!' roars my mum. 'And it's time that you stopped looking after everyone else and started looking after Sarah!'

William U's mum – Sarah – looks at my mum like William U's just been made Star of the Decade.

'You're right!' she says, drinking some more not-orange-juice. 'You're absolutely right! I'm not just Richard's wife and William U's mum! I'm Sarah Underwood! Lawyer! Traveller! Dancer!'

'Well, what are you waiting for?' says Rita,

standing up and wobbling a bit. 'Let's dance!'

Rita and William U's— and Sarah get up and start doing Mum Dancing, which is basically wiggling your bottom a lot. Lots of the other mums come up and start joining them. Even my mum gets up, although she can't wiggle her bottom that much because of her big tummy. They all look super happy. That's nice.

'Muuuum!' William U starts wailing. 'Muuuuuum – I want to go on the zip wire NOW, but Darcy says we have to wait our turn and it's going to be ages …'

Uh-oh.

Something's Upsetting William.

Here we go …

Sarah stops dancing and takes a big breath.

'William,' she says. 'You need to take your turn with the other children. If you don't like the way they're doing it, go and find something else to do.

You're a big boy. You sort it out.'

And with that, she turns around and carries on wiggling her bottom with Rita and the other mums.

'Oh,' says William U, looking slightly confused. 'Okay then …'

And he goes back to the zip wire and stands in the queue with everybody else.

'SCARLETT!!!!!!!'

I jump as high as the climbing frame (*simile*) and turn around to see who is screaming at me. It's Maisie. And she's so excited, her red glasses are nearly falling off. She grabs me and starts speaking so fast I can hardly hear her.

'Forever family … next week … St Lidwina's … Rosa … Amara…'

'Maisie, slow down!' I say, my heart beginning to get a bit excited. 'What's happened?'

'YOUR AUNTIES!' Maisie screams. 'Your

aunties are going to be my new foster family! My foster mum just told me! I can stay at St Lidwina's! We can still be School BFFs! In fact, it's better than that! We are going to be … COUSINS!'

'What?' I say, looking up as Aunty Rosa and Aunty Amara come towards us, holding hands with tears in their eyes. 'But I thought … the paperwork … the divorce … ?'

'Oh, Scarlett,' says Aunty Amara, giving me one of her lovely hugs. 'Is that what you thought? No – we're not getting divorced! We've been getting approved to be foster parents! We want to build our family! We're going to foster Maisie! And if she's happy living with us – we want to be her Forever Family!'

I look at Maisie, whose red glasses are full of tears. Or maybe my eyes are full of tears. Someone's eyes are full of tears anyway, but not sad ones – SUPER MASSIVE HAPPY ONES!

All right, crying. You can have two **BIG FEELINGS** after all.

'And even better,' Maisie pants. 'Rosa and Amara have said that MR NIBBLES CAN COME AND LIVE WITH US TOO!!!'

This is AMAZING! Maisie's found a Forever Family! Mr Nibbles has found a Forever Family! Maisie and Mr Nibbles and Polly and me are all going to be part of the same Forever Family!

I scream (*a lot*), then hug Maisie (*a lot*), then Polly comes over and we all scream together (*a lot*) and hug each other (*a lot*) and dance around like the wiggly-bottom mums (*a lot*), then everyone starts asking what's going on and we tell them and there's loads more screaming and hugging and dancing and I think I'm so happy I'm going to burst and—

'Excuse me!'

A loud voice shouts through the screaming and the hugging and the dancing. It's my mum. And she's standing in a puddle.

'Emi, are you okay?' Jakub asks her.

'I'm fine,' says my mum, holding the table with one hand and her tummy with the other. 'But it's time.'

'Time for what?' says Jakub, looking at his watch.

My mum smiles.

'Time for you to become a daddy,' she says. 'The babies are On Their Way.'

Well, all the mums start going utterly bonkers, making her sit down and bringing her glasses of water and telling her to breathe (*which is a bit silly, by the way, as she was breathing perfectly well already*), while Jakub goes very pale and starts shaking a bit.

'Okay!' he shouts. 'Nobody panic! Everything is fine! We're going to have a baby – two babies! It's all okay! DON'T PANIC!!!!'

My dad puts his arm around Jakub.

'I'll bring the car round,' he smiles, putting his orange juice down. 'I'll drive you. That way you can take care of Emi. You just stay here with her.'

'Okay … what … yes … um …' Jakub stutters before running over to Mum. 'EMI! Oh my days, EMI! Are you okay?! Can I get you anything?! Please stay calm! EVERYONE, JUST STAY CALM!!'

Felix's dads come over to Jakub, make him sit down, bring him a glass of water and tell him to breathe. (*This time I think that's actually very helpful, by the way.*)

Rita gives my mum a squeeze.

'I'll take a taxi home with the girls,' she says. 'Call me when there's news.'

'Okay,' says my mum, who is panting a lot for someone who is just sitting down. She reaches out and holds my hand.

'Are you ready to become a big sister?' she smiles at me.

'Not really,' I tell her, because you shouldn't tell lies. She laughs.

'You're going to be the best big sister ever,' Mum says, breathing out really hard and holding her tummy. I think she's got a tummy ache. She probably ate too much ice cream. 'I love you, Scarlett.'

'I love you, Mum,' I tell her, giving her a big hug. I can feel the babies kicking in her tummy. I hope they enjoyed the ice cream too. Looks like I can ask them myself very soon.

We hear my dad's car horn and Jakub helps

Mum up and takes her to the car.

'Good luck!' everyone shouts behind them. 'Congratulations!'

Rita comes over and gives me a big hug.

'I think we'd better have some more ice cream, don't you?' she winks.

She's *definitely* not been drinking orange juice.

I look over at Maisie sitting with my aunties, giggling away happily as they plan her bedroom in my aunties' Big Posh House. By next week, I'm going to have two new babies, a … hamster-in-law … and Maisie will be my cousin.

Yes.

I think this definitely deserves some more ice cream.

ChaPTer 15 + 0

Things I didn't know about babies

1) They do green poos (*like poorly pigeons*)
2) They eat and sleep ALL the time (*like Jakub*)
3) They're super cute (*like me*)

So I have a new brother and a new sister. They are called Reggie and Nancy. They are very little and very pink and very, very loud.

It's been just over a week since the twins were born and everyone is coming over today to 'wet the babies' heads'. I don't really understand why as we just gave them a bath this morning, but everyone seems very excited about it. We are in the new conservatory, which actually got finished!

(*My mum wanted to do a loft conversion too, by the way, but the builders said they were busy for the next three years.*)

Aunty Rosa and Aunty Amara are already here with Maisie, who is staying with them for the first time and Polly just arrived with my dad and Rita. I'm going back to Dad's tonight and Polly and I are going to sleep in the garden IN A TENT!!! (*One of the good things about having new brothers and sisters, by the way, is that all the adults want to make me happy all the time. And I've got LOADS of presents too.*)

'Is Lady Tottington-Snoot still coming?' Mum asks, tapping baby Nancy over her shoulder to make her burp (*Nancy does the most enormous burps, by the way – she's like my dad after Mexican food*).

'No – she's on an art retreat in Tuscany with Sadie and Sheila,' says Aunty Amara. 'They've all become great friends – I think they're going to a music festival next month.'

I smile. I'm glad Lady Tottington-Snoot has some friends. I know it'll make her playdates more fun.

I'll warn her about Hungry Hippos, though.

There's a knock at the door.

'Sorry to bother you, Jakub,' says Grumpy Barry. 'But is it okay if I start on the herb garden?'

(*Grumpy Barry is now working for Jakub as his assistant, by the way. It was my idea and it got Barry out from under Sheila's feet and got me a huge bag of sweets out of Jakub's secret stash, which was really good.*)

'Of course,' smiles Jakub, who is changing baby Reggie's nappy, just as a big fountain of wee comes out of my baby brother. 'But you've done more than enough today. Go home whenever you please.'

'I'm fine for a bit,' Grumpy Barry smiles.

'I'm … I'm enjoying myself.'

'Well then, you carry on,' says Jakub, putting a clean nappy on Reggie before he can pee all over him again and throwing the dirty one in the nappy bin. 'Come on over for some cake when you're done.'

'Will do,' smiles Grumpy Barry. 'Hi, girls.'

He waves at me and Maisie and Polly and we wave back. Perhaps Barry's not so Grumpy any more.

We'll find out when we camp out in the back garden tonight.

'Rita, would you mind holding Reggie for me?' Jakub asks.

'I'm dying to!' says Rita, taking Reggie in her arms and grinning at him. 'Being here is giving me ideas …'

She looks at my dad, who winks back. They must be planning a conservatory.

'Scarlett, will you come with me for a minute?' Jakub asks. I follow him out of the room. Now we've got so many babies, Mum and Jakub need my help, so I expect they want me to bring something in or wash something up or—

NO WAY!!!!!!

Jakub smiles proudly at the back door as I look out into the garden.

'IT'S MY TREEHOUSE!!!' I scream as I run outside. It is the best treehouse EVER, with a rope swing and a slide and an upstairs and a downstairs and it's white and red with a blue door and a green roof and now Polly and Maisie have come outside too and we've already decided it's our secret clubhouse and we're going to have a sleepover in it with sweets and I'm so excited that I realise I need to go back and hug Jakub and say thank you a gazillion times until he bursts.

'Whoa!' he says, hugging me back. 'So you like it?'

'I love it!' I squeal, running back to Polly and Maisie so we can play in our awesome treehouse.

We stay out there for ages, swinging and sliding and making plans, until it's getting a bit dark and it's time to go inside for cake.

Jakub has already poured all the grown-ups a glass of Bubbly Mummy Juice and a new bottle is sitting on the table. Reggie and Nancy are in a baby basket on the floor, but they're not very happy about it. The twins don't really like being in their basket; they like cuddles. So Reggie starts to cry, which makes his sister start to cry and they're both going very red-faced and screwing their little fists up and suddenly …

POP!!!!

The cork bursts out of the Bubbly Mummy Juice bottle, making a fountain in the middle of the room. I look back at Reggie and Nancy, who have decided to suck their hands instead.

'Wow!' laughs Jakub. 'We really did wet the babies' heads!'

I look at Maisie and Polly, and Polly and Maisie look at me. We all smile. The babies made the cork pop!

It looks like my brother and sister have some BIG FEELINGS too.

'A toast!' says Jakub, raising his glass. 'To our wonderful family.'

All the adults raise their glasses, and me and Polly and Maisie raise our cans of cola, because we're allowed them on special occasions. I look around the room. There's my mum, Jakub and Reggie and Nancy. There's my dad, Rita and Polly. There's my Aunty Rosa, Aunty Amara and Maisie. I really do have a super brilliant family.

And a really cool treehouse.

Another BIG FEELING starts to grow inside me. But this one isn't Angry Bubbles, or Worry

Wobbles or The Crying. This is something different. It's swimming around my whole body, making me warm and tingly and it's bright and colourful and loud and I'm not sure how I'm going to keep it in because I'm just so very, very …

WHIZZZZ!!!

POP!!!

BANG!!!

We all rush to the window to see the fireworks that have mysteriously filled the sky.

'Who did that?' Jakub asks with a smile.

I look at my brilliant family.

I did it.

Because I'm just so very, very …

HAPPY!!!

ACKNOWLEDGEMENTS

Well, I have some very **BIG FEELINGS** about coming to the end of Scarlett's adventures – and if I don't talk about them properly, it might start to rain, so …

Thank you, thank you, thank you a kerbillion times over to Chris Jevons for bringing Scarlett and her world so beautifully to life. It has been a joy and a pleasure working with you and if we don't create books together again, surely Evans 'n' Jevons has a future as a pop duo? You are a shining star.

To everyone at Hachette for their time, energy and support, especially the luminous Rachel Wade, who has been the most wonderful editor for this series. It's been emotional, friends.

This adventure is dedicated to five incredible educators, who have championed my books since my earliest days as an author. Schools do the most incredible work, not always under the easiest conditions, and deserve our love and thanks always. Ashley, Scott, Steph, Chris and Ian – thank you on behalf of all of us who have been lucky enough to cross your paths.

And finally, this story brought more than a little bit of The Crying up my throat as I thought of my own beloved grandmother, Audrey Andrews. In a family of scientists and engineers, my grandma and I were the only two dreamers. She nurtured me and my writing in so many ways and I think it's no coincidence that I was accepted by my agent

the day Grandma went on to her next adventure. Thank you, Grandma. I was blessed to have you.

To my family and friends, you are everything, always. And to my readers ... you are simply the best.

All my love,
Maz
xxx